"What are you doing?"

"This." He gently turned Molly to face him and took her into his arms.

Molly had known from the moment she'd agreed to show him some property that this was going to happen. Truth be told, she wanted it to happen.

There was a breathless moment when reality seemed to fade away, so that nothing remained in the universe besides the two of them—a man and a woman who'd been fated to come together in this time and place.

His mouth toyed with hers, and she went from aroused to hungry in a heartbeat. She might have fled Perry's Cove years ago, but now she was glad she'd stayed. Because she'd met Mark Ramsey. She'd known him only a few days, and he'd told her nothing about himself, yet incredibly his embrace felt like a homecoming. Reckless and not caring, she stepped closer to him and raised her face to his, ready for the kiss she felt was years overdue.

Abruptly Mark pulled away, looking tortured. "I tried to stay away from you. I told myself it would be better if I—"

But nothing had ever felt better to Molly. She silenced his protest with another k...

Dear Harlequin Intrigue Reader,

We have a thrilling summer lineup for this month and throughout the season to make your beach reading positively sizzle!

To start things off with a big splash, you won't want to miss the next installment in bestselling author Rebecca York's popular 43 LIGHT STREET series. An overturned conviction gives a hardened hero a new name, a new face and the means, motive and opportunity to close in on the real killer. But will his quest for revenge prevent him from becoming *Intimate Strangers* with the woman who fuels his every fantasy?

Reader favorite Debra Webb will leave you on the edge of your seat with the continuation of her ongoing series COLBY AGENCY. In *Her Secret Alibi,* a lethally sexy undercover agent will stop at nothing in the name of justice, only to fall under the mesmerizing spell of his prime suspect!

The heat wave continues with Julie Miller's next tantalizing tale in THE TAYLOR CLAN. When the one woman whom a smoldering arson investigator can't stop wanting becomes the target of a stalker, will *Kansas City's Bravest* battle an inferno of danger—and desire—in the name of love? And in *Sarah's Secrets* by Lisa Childs, shocking secret agendas ignite perilous sparks between a skittish single mom and a cynical tracker!

If you're in the mood for breathtaking romantic suspense, you'll be riveted by our selections this month!

Enjoy!

Denise O'Sullivan
Senior Editor
Harlequin Intrigue

INTIMATE STRANGERS

REBECCA YORK

RUTH GLICK WRITING AS REBECCA YORK

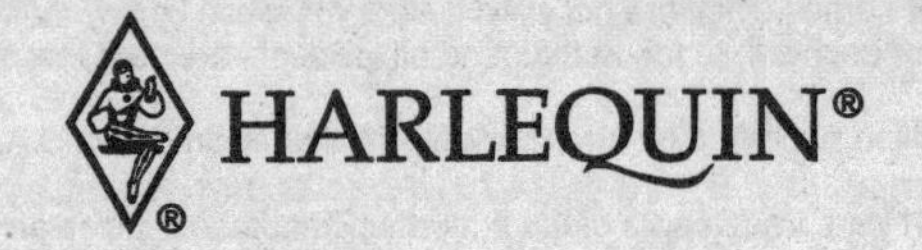

TORONTO • NEW YORK • LONDON
AMSTERDAM • PARIS • SYDNEY • HAMBURG
STOCKHOLM • ATHENS • TOKYO • MILAN • MADRID
PRAGUE • WARSAW • BUDAPEST • AUCKLAND

ISBN 0-373-22717-5

INTIMATE STRANGERS

This edition published by arrangement with Harlequin Books S.A.

Visit us at www.eHarlequin.com

Printed in U.S.A.

ABOUT THE AUTHOR

Award-winning, bestselling novelist Ruth Glick, who writes as Rebecca York, is the author of close to eighty books, including her popular 43 LIGHT STREET series for Harlequin Intrigue. Ruth says she has the best job in the world. Not only does she get paid for telling stories, she's also the author of twelve cookbooks. Ruth and her husband, Norman, travel frequently, researching locales for her novels and searching out new dishes for her cookbooks.

Books by Rebecca York

HARLEQUIN INTRIGUE

143—LIFE LINE*
155—SHATTERED VOWS*
167—WHISPERS IN THE NIGHT*
179—ONLY SKIN DEEP*
188—BAYOU MOON
193—TRIAL BY FIRE*
213—HOPSCOTCH*
233—CRADLE AND ALL*
253—WHAT CHILD IS THIS?*
273—MIDNIGHT KISS*
289—TANGLED VOWS*
298—TALONS OF THE FALCON†
301—FLIGHT OF THE RAVEN†
305—IN SEARCH OF THE DOVE†
318—TILL DEATH US DO PART*
338—PRINCE OF TIME*
407—FOR YOUR EYES ONLY*
437—FATHER AND CHILD*
473—NOWHERE MAN*
500—SHATTERED LULLABY*
534—MIDNIGHT CALLER*
558—NEVER TOO LATE*
606—BAYOU BLOOD BROTHERS
"Tyler"
625—THE MAN FROM TEXAS**
633—NEVER ALONE**
641—LASSITER'S LAW**
667—FROM THE SHADOWS*
684—GYPSY MAGIC
"Alessandra"
706—PHANTOM LOVER*
717—INTIMATE STRANGERS*

*43 Light Street
**43 Light Street: Mine To Keep
†The Peregrine Connection

Dear Reader,

Earlier this year I spent a relaxing week on the Outer Banks of North Carolina at a little beach town nestled among the sand dunes.

I loved the area, and decided I wanted to set a book there.

Of course, when I write a book, a picturesque little town becomes the setting for a murder conspiracy. So I changed the name to Perry's Cove, to protect the innocent.

In my story, Mike Randall was convicted of his wife's murder and went to prison. But thanks to the Light Street Foundation, he's been exonerated. Now he wants to make sure the real killer pays. So he's come back to the scene of the crime with a new name, Mark Ramsey, and a new face.

But the murder investigation is complicated by his feelings for Molly Dumont, a woman he was drawn to during the years of his failing marriage. Mike and Molly would never have acted on their feelings while they were married to other people. Although they're both free now, the emotional bond growing between them gets tangled up in Mark's murder investigation. Is Molly involved, or is she also an innocent bystander? What will happen when she finds out that Mark has been lying to her since arriving in town? And will they live long enough to explore the depths of the passion their reunion generates?

These are some of the questions I've asked and answered in *Intimate Strangers*.

Sincerely,

Ruth

Ruth Glick writing as Rebecca York

CAST OF CHARACTERS

Mike Randall—He came back to Perry's Cove with a hidden agenda.

Mark Ramsey—Mike's new name, to go with his new face.

Molly Dumont—Was she an innocent bystander, or was she involved in murder?

Larry Iverson—Why did he send Molly into danger?

Oliver Garrison—The antique dealer's blood pressure went up when Mike came back to town.

Bill Bauder—Did he report the news or make it?

Dean Hammer—Was the sheriff a good guy or a bad guy?

Cory Daniels—Did he have something personal against Mike Randall?

Doris Masters—She was Oliver Garrison's lover. Were they in a conspiracy together?

Jerry Tilden—Why were his construction projects plagued with accidents?

Prologue

The nightmare dug its talons into his flesh, seized him by the throat and choked off his breath. He knew it was just a dream, but he couldn't shake the sick, helpless feeling.

He was back in the living hell of the past five years. Back in prison, under the control of guards who considered him a member of a subhuman species. He was a convicted murderer, after all. And that gave them the right to subject him to any indignity they chose.

They were strip-searching him, making him bend over, probing the recesses of his body, as though they really thought they were going to find he was hiding a six-pack of beer that he intended to sell for enormous profits to the other inmates.

"You can go," Big Louie growled. He was one of the real sadists among them. A man who enjoyed inflicting humiliation—and pain, if he could get away with it.

The prisoner wanted to scream out that he wasn't guilty of anything beyond stupidity. But he knew that everyone claimed innocence, so he kept his mouth clamped shut, and simply stood there, breathing in the scent of stale sweat and urine, and the disinfectant that failed to mask them.

Then an electric gate opened, and someone gave him a push into the exercise yard. He stumbled forward, struggling to regain his footing, because if he fell on his face now, he was a dead man.

Cunningham was there, waiting for him to make the wrong move. Cunningham, who hated his guts because he used correct grammar, and was tough enough to defend himself. But today the guy had a knife he'd made from a piece of PVC pipe. It might not be metal, but it was honed to a fine point.

The guards were right on the other side of the gate. Though they must have seen the knife, they did nothing.

When the weapon came slashing toward him, he jumped back, his shoulders slamming against the wire fence.

Behind him, he heard Big Louie laugh. Maybe he'd set this up. Maybe he'd even placed a bet on Cunningham to win.

A curse sprang to the prisoner's lips as he tried to raise his hand to ward off another blow. But he couldn't move. Someone behind him had grabbed his arms. He struggled to twist away, but the unseen demons held him fast. And the knife came down, aiming for his heart.

He fought with all his strength, trying to wrest himself from the powerful grasp. And finally he realized that he was tangled in the bedclothes. That only a thin sheet was holding him down.

He flopped back against the mattress, carefully untangling his arms and legs as he dragged in drafts of the cool, clean night air wafting through the window.

The air-conditioning had been on when he'd first come into the hotel room, but he couldn't stand the feeling of being confined so he'd turned off the climate control and opened the window.

He swiped an arm across his forehead, feeling cold sweat. With a grimace, he heaved himself out of bed and made his way toward the bathroom. It was a large room—almost as large as the cell he'd shared with another inmate for five long years. But while the cell's toilet–sink combo in the corner had been institutional stainless steel, now he leaned over an expanse of gleaming marble countertop and turned on the water. When it was cold, he splashed some on his sweaty face, then cupped his hands under the stream and lifted them to his mouth.

The clean, modern bathroom was a luxury he hadn't quite gotten used to. Like the wide bed with its firm mattress. Or the television he could turn on anytime he wanted. Or the phone on the bedside table.

Every morning when he woke up, it was like a miracle. He was free. Thanks to hope, prayers and the Light Street Foundation.

He gripped the edge of the counter, his fingers digging into the hard surface. Then he slowly raised his gaze to the mirror. As it had for the past few months, the face staring back at him jarred his senses. Not his old face. An expensive new one. Acquired so he could come back to Perry's Cove and find the bastard who had taken away five years of his life.

Chapter One

"So now your life of lies and falsehoods officially begins," Mark Ramsey said aloud into the closed confines of the car as he pulled into a space near the waterfront.

The parking lot was free. The city council wanted to make it as easy as possible for visitors to enjoy the many charms of Perry's Cove, North Carolina.

He sat for a minute, taking shallow breaths, his hands gripping the wheel. He could still change his mind and walk away from this damn little town that had done its best to destroy him. But caving in had never been in his nature. He'd grown up a fighter and it was too late to change now.

So he climbed out of his secondhand Ford Taurus, then turned and pressed the remote that locked the doors.

Once, he might have skipped that safety precaution. Now he knew you couldn't be too careful in these little shore towns. They might look safe as a nun's virtue, but there were a lot of con artists walking around the streets.

Like himself, for example. The last time he'd been

in Perry's Cove, he'd been Mike Randall. Now he was back with his new name and his new face.

"You're Mark Ramsey," he murmured, just to hear the sound of the syllables. As he spoke, he raised his face to the blue sky and the sun. The feel of wind blowing back his dark hair was still a luxury he couldn't take for granted.

As if he could outrun the past, he strode quickly down the path from the parking lot to the waterfront. Long ago the main business in the area had been fishing. Now the town lived off the tourists who came to soak up the quaint atmosphere, shop for souvenirs and hit the beaches. Once, he had seen the place as charming. To his newly cynical eye, however, the storefronts looked like pretty little money traps.

The shopping center right on the water was a brand-new, three-story building. But across the street, most of the shops had been created from old residences. Businesses went in and out. He saw that the ladies' weaving guild had taken over the ground floor of a small clapboard house. Next door was a boutique in a converted Victorian. Down a bit, an antique shop he remembered was now a T-shirt emporium.

He could walk into any of those places and buy anything he wanted. The idea was still mind-blowing. When the gates of the federal pen had first locked him in, he'd been angry and determined to fight his conviction. A couple of years in the joint had drained the piss and vinegar out of him, and he'd gotten used to the reality that he was going to die in prison.

Then a ray of hope had opened up at the end of his long, dark tunnel. It still seemed like a miracle that he had his life back—minus those five very nasty years. Not his old life, of course. Despite the warmth of the sun, a wave of cold traveled over his skin as he thought about stepping back into the town that had convicted him of murder and thrown away the key.

Well, not the whole population. Surely there was someone here who hadn't thought he'd killed his wife and conveniently gotten rid of the body. Actually, there *was* someone who knew it wasn't true. The real murderer.

Mark Ramsey was going to track down the real killer and extract a substantial payment for years of pain and suffering. First, though, he needed to understand the lay of the land, because acting quickly could have fatal consequences.

He set his course for Today's Catch, the seafood restaurant where he'd enjoyed many a pleasant lunch in his previous life. Hopefully, the food was as good as he remembered. There hadn't been much seafood in prison, beyond canned tuna and the dried-out mystery fish he could never identify.

The eating establishment was a favorite spot for locals and tourists alike. A small boardwalk fronted the building, and along one side a covered deck supplied seating where diners could look out over both Main Street and the cove that had given the town its name.

The hostess looked up from her spot at the podium and swept back a fall of long brown hair. It was Callie Fletcher, a woman he'd known casually in town. Not well, but well enough that she might recognize him.

She paused a beat as she studied his face, and he felt his stomach clench as he waited for her to come out with his real name.

Instead, she blinked and simply said, "Can I help you?"

He kept his gaze steady on hers as he shoved one

hand casually into his pocket and answered, "I'd like a table in a quiet corner." Even his voice was different. It hadn't the same timbre as when he'd lived here, thanks to a prison fight in which he'd gotten a fist to the larynx.

He watched Callie taking in his muscular arms and shoulders, another new development. When he'd lived in town he hadn't exactly had a remarkable physique. Truth be told, he'd been starting to acquire a little bit of a paunch.

But in prison, where hardly any aspect of his life had been under his control, physical fitness had taken on importance. Using books from the library, he'd designed an exercise program and stuck to it religiously. The regimen wasn't just an ego trip. It had the practical result of making him less vulnerable to attacks from the sharks who preyed on the weak.

"Would you like to sit inside or out?" Callie asked, interrupting his thoughts.

"Outside," he answered, unconsciously filling his lungs with the salt air blowing off the cove.

Callie led him to a table topped by a green-and-white-striped umbrella, and he sat in the shade, stretching out his long legs and crossing them comfortably at the ankles as he picked up his menu and studied the selections.

He hoped he looked at ease. Truthfully, he hoped he could choke down lunch. Though his plans had seemed reasonable when he'd first made them, now he wondered if he could actually pull them off.

He studied the menu, decided on the fish of the day, then leaned back in his seat and took a sip of water.

He almost swallowed the wrong way when he saw

a short, balding man striding down the sidewalk as though he owned it.

Some people thought he did. Bill Bauder was the editor of the *Voice of Perry's Cove,* the local twice-weekly paper, and he had a hell of a lot of influence on public opinion in the community. The prudish editor had been convinced of Mike Randall's guilt. He'd written editorials congratulating the police for removing the snake from their midst, and he'd kept whipping up public opinion against the wife murderer, as if he'd had a personal stake in the outcome of the trial.

Bauder was on his shortlist of murder suspects. Perhaps it was an omen that the editor was one of the first familiar faces Mark saw in town.

His chest tightened as he watched Bauder turn in at the restaurant entrance, then follow Callie inside. Mark toyed with the idea of walking past the man's table on the way to the rest room, so he could test his new face on a well-known enemy. If Bill Bauder didn't recognize him, nobody would. Then he reminded himself there was no hurry. He was going to be here for a while.

He sent another mental note of thanks to the Light Street Foundation. Without them, he'd still be rotting in his cell.

Because of his educational background, he'd worked in the prison library, where he'd read the *Washington Post* every morning. In the feature section, he'd seen an article about how the foundation was reopening a select few felony cases, thanks to a guy named Lucas Somerville, who himself had once been falsely accused of murder and robbery. Somerville had given them a wad of money to help people in similar circumstances.

Mark—he was careful to think of himself as Mark now—had had all the time in the world to compose a long, well-written letter, explaining that his lawyer had done a pretty poor job of refuting the circumstantial case against him. Veronica's body had never been found. But when she disappeared, her parents came forward and told the police that she'd been having problems with her husband.

Actually, he and Veronica had been on a speeding train headed for a divorce. But he hadn't killed her. He'd thought he had nothing to hide, so he'd let the police search his home and office. Somebody had planted a bloody shirt and a pair of slacks in his tool room. And the blood was Veronica's type.

After that, the cops had come down heavily on the failing marriage and the very public fight he and Veronica had had the night she disappeared. And on the million-dollar insurance policy he was supposed to have taken out on her life. They didn't believe he'd known nothing about the policy until the company had notified him.

The mound of evidence had been enough for the state to win a murder conviction and a life sentence.

But Dan Cassidy, a lawyer who volunteered at the Light Street Foundation, went back to the bloody clothing and forced the court to order DNA testing, comparing the blood to cells from Veronica's hair, which had been taken from among her things in her family's place in New Jersey. They didn't match. Since her body had never been found, that pulled the linchpin out of the state's case.

Cassidy was very persuasive—about the evidence and about the inadequacy of the previous defense lawyer. After some pro forma protests, the state turned

Mike Randall loose. As soon as he walked through the penitentiary gates and heard them hiss shut behind him, he started planning his return engagement in Perry's Cove to find out who had set him up.

He touched his hand to his face, just a quick touch as he marveled once again at the wonders of modern science. One of the first things he did after getting out of prison was visit a top plastic surgeon. Dr. Hamilton was an artist with his knife. He'd changed Mike Randall into Mark Ramsey—a man who bore little resemblance to the guy who'd spent five years in prison.

Unlike most ex-cons who came out of the joint penniless and unable to cope with life in the real world, Mark had money. Light Street Foundation had set him up with one hundred thousand dollars, and once the murder conviction was overturned, he collected on that million-dollar insurance policy.

Lunch arrived, and Mark dug in, savoring the flavor of the snapper. In his old life he'd taken good food for granted. Now he appreciated every bite.

As he ate, he looked out across the street to a building being renovated. Apparently one of the shops was getting a complete face-lift, including new cedar shingles, trim and new roof.

He could see workmen moving around on the roof, and he watched as he ate his lunch.

A sign leaned against the bottom of the front wall beside the two front steps. It said the Calico Duck.

The cute name should bring in the tourists, but the merchandise would determine whether they parted with some of their cash.

When he'd lived in Perry's Cove, he'd owned a contractor business, so his interest in the construction was more than casual. He would have finished the roof before setting up the scaffolding on the front. But probably the shop owner was in a hurry to get things completed. After lunch he resisted the tempting offerings on the dessert tray. He liked his new body, and he had no intention of letting it go to fat.

One of his next stops would be one of the real estate offices at the edge of town to look for a rental where he'd have enough space for some home-gym equipment. He planned to tell everyone that he was an author who had come to Perry's Cove seeking peace and quiet to finish a book.

In fact, that wasn't a lie. He *was* planning a book—about his experiences as a man wrongfully imprisoned for murder. But there was no way to end the book until he unraveled the mystery of who had murdered Veronica Randall.

He paid his bill with the new credit card he'd acquired in the name of Mark Ramsey. In fact, he had bought a whole set of credentials: social security card, birth certificate and a good credit rating to go along with his new gold and platinum cards. Fingerprints would be a problem, of course. But he didn't intend leaving them anywhere it would make a difference.

Interested in the work on the building he'd been looking at, he walked across the street, then into an interior courtyard. The sound of a car door slamming snared his attention, and he stopped dead in his tracks when he realized who had pulled into the parking pad in back of the new construction site. He caught only a glance of her blond hair through the car window, but he was sure it was Molly Dumont.

He'd thought he was prepared to come back here and face the past, but suddenly he felt as if he'd been punched in the gut. If picturing Bill Bauder in hell had helped him wile away the endless hours behind bars, Molly had provided quite different fantasies. In the tough, all-male environment of the cell block, he'd fallen asleep imagining what he and Molly Dumont could do in bed together. And her presence had carried over into the wild, erotic dreams there had been no way to repress.

He could have chosen any woman in the world for his favorite partner. In fact, in his narrow prison bunk, he'd imagined himself making love with models and movie actresses. But he'd always come back to Molly because his memories of her were more real, more vital than any of the false images from American popular culture. In prison, when he'd thought he was never going to see her again, he'd had no hesitation investing a lot of emotional and creative energy in their fantasy encounters.

Seeing her in person, he realized she was going to be a complication he didn't need.

He'd known her for two years before his murder conviction, when they'd both been married. Even back then, he'd thought about what his life would be like with her instead of the shrew his wife had become. But he hadn't done anything about it. Illicit relationships weren't his style. Nor was breaking up someone else's apparently stable marriage.

As far as he knew, she was still with Phil, but that didn't stop his heart from beating faster as he watched her get out of the car, didn't stop the hitch in his throat as she walked gracefully toward the front of the shop, her wheat-colored hair blowing back from her delicate face.

He got only a profile view of her features, screened by that curtain of thick hair. Then her back was to him, but his mind filled in the rest. Her blue eyes, her straight nose and her sensuous lips had been branded on his consciousness.

Could she possibly be as beautiful as he'd remembered? He needed to find out. He figured he was going to run into her some time. No time like the present to gauge how she reacted to him.

He knew he was rationalizing. He knew he was making up excuses for embarking on a risky course of action. He had no business approaching her. It wasn't necessary, unless she turned out to be involved in... What?

A conspiracy against him?

He hated to think in those terms. Somehow, he'd rather it be just one person who had a beef against him and Veronica. Enough of a beef to kill her and pin the murder on her unsuspecting husband. Still, he couldn't dismiss the possibility that he was up against something bigger.

But what?

He was going to find out—without getting tangled up with Molly Dumont. That very wise decision didn't stop him from walking closer to the parking pad.

He had stopped several feet from the car when movement on the roof of the shop caught his attention. Someone was peering over the edge, looking down at Molly.

He'd seen the workmen leave, probably for lunch. But now one of them was back, a guy wearing blue coveralls and a navy cap pulled down over his face.

Mark thought that maybe the guy was going to call out to her so she'd know he was up there. But he said nothing, and there was something strange about the way he moved with slow deliberation, as if he wasn't comfortable up there.

Then suddenly the man seemed to stumble. His foot shot awkwardly to the side, hitting a large metal container sitting too near the edge of the roof. It was filled with something heavy, Mark could tell by the way it rocked back and forth, teetering on the edge of disaster just as Molly marched up the back sidewalk toward the door, oblivious of what was going on above her.

Mark watched the unfolding drama in horror. The bucket wobbled again, and he knew it was going over the edge, its trajectory on a collision course with the woman below.

Chapter Two

"Molly, watch out!" he shouted. At the same time he launched himself with lightning reflexes across the space that separated them. With milliseconds to spare, he caught her in an upper-body tackle and threw her off the walkway, just as the metal bucket hit the sidewalk with an earsplitting crash.

But the bulk of his attention was focused on Molly, who gasped as she landed under him on the ground.

Thank God he'd angled them toward a clear patch of grass, otherwise she might have come down on construction debris.

For long seconds neither one of them moved, probably because they were both too stunned by the impact. Still, his mind was registering familiar sensations. As he lay there on top of her, he realized that it had been years since he'd gotten this close to a woman, his body crushed to hers, separated by only a few layers of clothing.

He wanted to press himself more tightly against Molly's feminine curves. But that way lay madness. Instead he shifted his weight to the side, keeping his arms protectively around her.

The emergency's over. Turn her loose, he ordered

himself. *Before you give away the whole show.* But now that he held her in his embrace, his body wouldn't obey the command from his brain.

The shock of clasping a living, breathing woman was overwhelming. Not just any woman. *This* woman. Of all the ones with whom he could have made first contact after the long years of living inside his own head, it was Molly. He was instantly rock hard, his whole body taut and ready for action.

He'd come out of the pen thinking that now he could have all the things he'd been denied for years, starting with a sixteen-ounce strip steak and sex. The steak had been no problem. Sex was another matter.

Maybe, before he'd given himself a chance to think too deeply, he should have picked up some likely candidate in a bar. But there were reasons why he hadn't done it. He'd felt tainted then. Felt as though the sour smell of prison was oozing out of his pores. So he'd kept his distance from the females of the species and focused on the other facets of daily life that were new and strange to him—like waking up and going to bed when he wanted, buying clothing and picking a different delicacy every night for dinner.

Then he'd gone in for surgery, and his face had looked as if he'd been pounded by Mike Tyson for fifteen rounds. That had automatically disqualified him from any intimate contact.

Now here he was holding Molly Dumont.

Turn her loose, he told himself again. But his muscles still failed to obey the command, and he realized in that moment that he was more needy than he'd dreamed possible.

The sudden feeling of vulnerability was like a

crushing blow to the chest. At least it did something to deflate his arousal.

He'd told himself that his dreams of Molly had no relationship to reality, and in a way that was true. The dreams had served him up an image that was devastatingly sexual.

In the flesh, she was even more devastating.

A host of sensations swamped his senses. Her scent enveloped him—the delicate aroma of soap and flowers and woman. His face brushed her soft cheek. And as he stared into the blue of her eyes, he felt as though he would drown in their depths.

The totality of her only increased the sexual awareness. One of her breasts pressed against his side, and he was vividly aware of that very feminine combination of softness and fullness.

Perhaps she heard his sharp intake of breath, because she was the one who pulled away, those blue eyes alive with questions. Her pretty lips parted, but she remained silent, just looking at him.

He wanted to scramble up and run. But he managed to stay where he was and say in the new gravelly voice he'd acquired, "Are you all right?"

The question seemed to bring her out of a trance. She blinked, then moved her arms and legs, taking a silent inventory. "I think so. What happened? You came out of nowhere and knocked me down."

"Yeah. Sorry. I saw something falling off the roof. You were going to walk right under it."

"I heard it hit." She turned her head, breaking the eye contact with him, and he grappled with a sudden sense of loss.

She stared at the metal can and the dark shingles scattered around it, before her gaze came back to his.

"It would have been pretty bad if that thing had landed on me."

"Yeah."

She tipped her head to one side as she continued to study him. "There's something so familiar about you. Do I know you?"

"No!" His answer came out too sharp and too quick.

Her tongue flicked out, stroking across her bottom lip, as though he'd convinced her of just the opposite.

He stood up abruptly, thinking he should offer her his hand. But she was already pushing herself up. Bending, she brushed her hands across the streaks of dirt on her dark skirt, slapping at it with only partial success.

He might have offered to help, but he kept his own hands at his sides.

When she raised her head again, it was to study him with unnerving intensity. "Are you sure we haven't met?"

He wanted to clamp his teeth together, but somehow he kept his jaw relaxed. "I'd remember if we had."

"Yes." She said it slowly, agreeing with him. Then she delivered a punch to his guts, "You called my name."

"What?"

"When that thing was falling off the roof, you called out to me. You called me by name."

"No." He shook his head in denial, then added, "How could I have?"

Damn. He wasn't as good at deception as he'd thought he'd be. First he'd instinctively used her name when he saw she was in danger. Now he was jumping in with both feet to issue a denial.

He turned his head toward the can lying bent and twisted on the sidewalk, changing the subject with deliberate speed. "I'm wondering what that big container was doing up on the roof."

"They're remodeling the shop."

"Who?"

"Tilden's."

He nodded. Tilden's had been his chief rival back in the old days when he'd been on the success treadmill, bidding on every project that came along. Sometimes he'd get the job; sometimes they did. Their work was okay, but he didn't think much of their estimating abilities. Or maybe Jerry Tilden had lowballed him on purpose.

She was watching his expression, as if seeing the wheels turning in his head. "You know the company?" she asked.

"No," he answered, another denial, another lie. The words tumbling out of his mouth didn't feel natural on his tongue, but he'd known all along that if he came here looking for the murderer, he was going to have to do a lot of prevaricating. But now he was being forced into lying to Molly Dumont—and he felt like a rat.

He directed the discussion back to the aborted disaster. "A workman was up there. I saw him catch his foot on the bucket or give it a push."

"Not on purpose!"

"Let's hope not."

"Why would anyone do that?"

He shrugged, then stood and walked to the metal can where heavy shingles had spilled out onto the ground, nasty missiles that would have done a lot of damage raining down on human flesh.

An involuntary shudder traveled over his skin. If that bucket had ended up on the edge of the roof by mistake, it was a pretty serious safety breach. If not...then what had been the motive?

"Do you want me to go up there and have a look?" he asked on impulse.

She stood for a moment, staring off into the distance, then swung her gaze back to him. "I think you're assuming that I'm having this shop renovated for myself."

"You're not?"

"This isn't my place. I'm looking in on the project for Shoreside Realty. A client is fixing up the property for sale."

"Oh." He tried to fit the answer into the facts he remembered. Five years ago Molly Dumont and her husband had owned an antique business. They and a group of other dealers, including Veronica, had banded together to buy an old seafood-processing building. Mark had done the conversion himself, turning the large space into an antique gallery with about a half-dozen businesses under the same roof. The place was called the Treasure Hunt Pavilion. When he'd seen Molly outside the Calico Duck, he'd assumed that the Dumonts had been doing well enough to expand into their own space.

But he could hardly go into any of that background now—or ask why she'd changed her profession when she'd been so good at fixing up and selling old furniture and decorative pieces. He settled for, "Shoreside Realty? I was going to stop over at their office."

It was her turn to say, "Oh?"

He shifted his weight from one foot to the other. "I'm thinking of renting a house in the area for several months, and I want to find out what's available.'' In the next breath, he heard himself asking, ''Would you be interested in handling that for me?''

WOULD SHE? Molly hesitated a beat before answering. Lord knows, she needed the money. She'd only gotten her real estate license within the past two years, and she was finding that it was either feast or famine. When you made a sale, you got a very nice commission. But you could spend days taking clients around with no results. And then there was the problem of listings. You got the best commissions when you were the agent who had signed up the property. Otherwise, you had to split the money.

Although she hated the cutthroat aspects of the business, she loved helping people find the perfect home or helping clients ready their property for sale. Just the way she'd once loved selling people items they'd cherish for years when she'd been an antique dealer.

Signing up a renter wouldn't bring in the same bucks as selling a home, but the money could help tide her over until she sold one of the properties she was working on now.

So why was she hesitating?

For personal reasons. She was flustered. And embarrassed that she'd felt a spurt of attraction for this stranger—attraction she didn't want to feel. She was a good judge of people—she had to be in her profession—and she was pretty sure that at the core, her rescuer was a good man. Yet she sensed he had a hidden agenda, that he wasn't being entirely straight with her.

Stalling, she considered his question for several seconds, then asked, ''A rental, you say? What's your interest in the area?'' She flexed and unflexed her right hand. Earlier she hadn't noticed that she'd scraped it when she'd hit the ground. Now it was starting to sting.

''I'm writing a book. I want a location with no distractions where I can get a lot of work done.''

''Where are you staying?''

''The East Point Lodge.''

Not a shabby address, she thought. ''What price range are you looking for?''

''I've saved up a fair amount of money from, uh, the advance. I can afford something nice. But I'm not in the market for one of those million-dollar beach houses. Something small and cozy.''

''Okay.''

''You'll help me out?'' he clarified.

''Yes.'' She paused. ''You want something on the beach?''

''It would depend on the house. I'm not all that familiar with Perry's Cove. I assume beach houses are expensive.''

He'd said that last part casually enough, yet she got the feeling maybe he knew more about the area than he was letting on. But why would he want to hide that knowledge?

Probably she should turn him over to one of the guys, who wouldn't have to worry about personal involvement with an attractive male client. Instead she asked, ''When do you want to start?''

''No time like the present.''

''All right. But I have to finish up here.'' She started toward the door, then stopped abruptly and gestured toward the crumpled metal container. ''I'm sorry. I'm not quite myself at the moment. I'm Molly Dumont,'' she said, watching him closely and wondering again about the moment before the accident when she'd thought she'd heard her name. Maybe it had been her guardian angel calling.

"What are you thinking?" he asked.

She wondered what expression had flickered across her face. "I was having a fantasy moment."

"Oh, yeah?"

He sounded too interested, and she made a note not to ask him about his fantasies. "I was thinking maybe some spiritual protector was watching out for me and called out a warning."

"That's as good an explanation as any. Has that happened to you before?"

"Actually, no."

He absorbed that in the deliberate way he had of taking in information, then said, "I'm Mark Ramsey."

She felt a small flash of disappointment. The name wasn't familiar. But something about the sound of it—something about *him*—teased her memory. Not the voice, certainly. Something else. The way he stood? His eyes? She tried to hook her mind around the elusive detail, but it wiggled out of her grasp, leaving her with an edgy, unsettled feeling.

"I don't think you should go in there alone," he said in the gravelly voice that she found very attractive.

She had stepped onto the concrete pad at the back door. Now she stopped in midstride. "Why not?"

"There was an accident out here. There could be an accident inside."

As she thought about that, she tried not to make any more of his warning than its face value. This was a construction site, and things could happen; yet her boss, Larry Iverson, hadn't hesitated to send her here. So what was she going to do—call Larry and tell him to do his own inspecting? Not likely.

She stepped into the building and was aware of Mark Ramsey following behind.

In the back room, the walls had been stripped to the studs. When she turned, she saw Ramsey examining the workmanship, as though he were the general contractor—or maybe the building-code inspector.

"You know about construction?" she asked.

"Some." He strode past her and into the front room, which was filled with a jumble of discarded wood and other debris.

"Get a crew from Tilden's to clean this place up," he commented. "They shouldn't leave it like this. And be careful. There could be nails in that mess."

"Thanks." He'd remembered the name Tilden's, she noted. How many people would have filed that away?

Maybe it was a guy thing, like remembering the name of a sports team. When she slid him another contemplative glance, he was looking out the back door.

"This place is being remodeled on speculation?" he asked.

"Yes."

"So business is good in town."

"Good enough, I guess."

He looked as if he was dying to ask another question.

"What is it you want to know?" she prompted.

When he didn't answer, she added, "You're not thinking of setting up shop in town, are you?"

"No. I just want to make sure I'll have all the comforts here."

Without waiting for a reply, he stepped out the door again, avoiding more construction debris piled in the small backyard, then craned his neck up toward the roof. Without asking permission, he reached for the bottom rung of the scaffolding along the wall, pulled himself up and climbed toward the roof. He made it look easy, yet she'd seen guys who could barely get from one rung to the next without puffing. She mentally set down another fact about Mark Ramsey. He was strong.

He climbed onto the roof, his body making a sharp angle with the slanting surface. When he disappeared from sight, she held her breath. It was dangerous up there. The image of him tumbling to the ground sent a sudden wave of cold through her, and she squeezed her eyes shut to banish the frightening picture.

The reaction was strong, and she wondered why. She barely knew the man. But he'd saved her life. More than that, he'd risked his own life, she realized suddenly, fitting in a new piece of the Mark Ramsey puzzle. That bucket of shingles could have landed on him just as easily as on her, but he'd ignored his own safety to throw her out of the way.

Maybe that was why she was reacting so strongly to him, she decided, more strongly than she had to any man in a long time.

She stood there for another moment, staring at the roof, worrying about him. Then, with a shake of her head she ducked back inside and went into the little bathroom. There was a roll of paper towels sitting on the sink, and she wet one, using it to dab at the dirt streak on the front of her skirt. The small domestic job made her hand sting and she turned her palm up, looking at the reddened streak. She thrust it under the faucet, washing the scraped flesh. Perhaps the running water kept her from hearing Mark Ramsey come back.

At any rate, he was very close to her by the time she realized she wasn't alone. A small scream bubbled from her throat.

His apology was instantaneous. "I'm sorry. I didn't mean to scare you."

She whirled to face him, hearing the raw nerves in her voice as she asked, "What are you doing? Sneaking up on me?"

"I came down to give you the roof report. Are you all right?" His gaze was fixed on the hand she'd been washing. Reaching out, he grasped it, cradling it in his big palm as he looked down at the injury. All her attention centered on that contact—her small hand resting in his much larger one.

"You hurt yourself."

"It's not bad."

"Do you have any antiseptic?"

"No. Really, it's okay," she insisted. He kept her hand captive, or at least that was what it seemed like, for another few seconds during which she felt her heart rate accelerate.

The reaction embarrassed her, so she kept her gaze trained on her palm, unable to meet his eyes.

When she finally realized she had the power to pull away, she did. Turning, she snatched up another paper towel and started to rub her hand.

As she swung back to the man standing in the doorway, she told herself she was feeling more composed. "So, what did you find out?" she asked.

"Not much. They're putting on a new roof. The

materials are good quality. It should last for the next twenty years."

"And the bucket?"

"I have no idea why somebody left it like that. It was an accident waiting to happen. There was no one up there to ask. And I'll bet if you question Tilden's, you'll find out nobody knew nothing." His eyes turned flinty. "So who knew you were coming here?"

She blinked as she took in the implications. "My boss asked me to look in. I don't know who else he mentioned it to."

"What were you supposed to do here exactly?"

"I'm supposed to report on the progress of the work. He wants an estimate of how soon the shop will be ready to rent."

"Are you a construction expert?"

"No."

"Then you'd get a better estimate from the builder."

"He wanted to know what I think," she answered, instinctively defending Larry.

He nodded, but she could see he was making silent connections and judgments inside his head. "Has your boss gotten into any...fights lately? I mean, is there anyone who might have it in for him?"

She thought about that, wondering what she should say exactly. She knew stuff about Larry, but it was none of this man's business.

"Are there people who might have reasons to get back at him?" he pressed.

"I don't like talking about him."

"You wouldn't like a big bucket of shingles coming down on your head, either."

When he put it that way, the question called for a

response. "Larry has a quick temper. He's made some people around here angry. But why would that make someone go after me?"

"Do you have a personal relationship with him?"

The question was so inappropriate that she blinked. "Certainly not!"

He shoved his hands into his pockets, perhaps in a bid to look casual. But she could see the tension in his shoulders.

"I'm trying to help you. Don't get your back up."

"Why should you care about me?"

He paused a beat before answering, "I like you."

"You don't know me."

She saw him swallow, as though the retort had taken him off guard. "I'm a quick-impressions kind of guy."

"That's a useful talent."

"Look, if you're worried about me, I can give you references." He said it quickly, as if he really didn't want her to call him on that detail.

Probably she should tell him that she'd changed her mind about helping him find a place to live. But somehow the words stayed locked in her throat.

"I have to look around here. That's what I was sent over to do," she said instead.

"I'll get out of your way, then." He stepped back into the yard, leaving her to make a quick survey of the interior work. But it was difficult to focus on the state of the construction. She'd been thinking when she drove here that Larry had sent the wrong person, since she didn't know much about remodeling. She was even more uncomfortable with the assignment now, but she pulled out her notebook and wrote down what she saw. The interior wall studs were in place.

The insulation was on the exterior walls. Probably if she asked Mark Ramsey, he'd give her a time frame.

When she came back to the door, Ramsey was talking to a man who must be one of the construction workers.

From the sound of it, her rescuer was grilling him. "So you don't know anything about the bucket of shingles?" he pressed.

"That's what I told you."

"You have no idea how it fell from the roof?"

"I'm not working on the roof. I'm a carpenter."

"Right. Thanks for your help. You might want to tell your boss about what happened here." Ramsey turned and gestured toward the unguided missiles spread across the front walk.

"Yeah. Sure."

Molly walked outside just as the workman disappeared around the side of the building. "I should stop home and change my skirt."

"You look fine."

"I don't look very professional. I don't usually take clients out covered with dirt."

"We both know how your clothes got messed up."

"Nevertheless, I'll feel better after I change," she insisted, because she felt as though she was losing command of events, and this was one way she could exercise control. There was another factor, too. She needed to put some distance between herself and Mark Ramsey. If she didn't want to see him again, she could let another agent take the job.

"So, should we meet back at your office?" he asked as if he was following the drift of her thoughts.

"Yes." She looked at her watch. "In an hour," she added, thinking that two days would be more like it.

"It's on the north side of town, just before you reach the highway. On the right. You can't miss it."

As she turned and hurriedly walked to her car, she could feel Mark Ramsey's gaze burning into her back. But she kept herself from looking around as she got into the car and sped off.

Chapter Three

Mark watched Molly Dumont leave, wondering if she was really going to show up at the Shoreside office in an hour. He'd sensed her ambivalence about getting back together—and his own ambivalence, if he were brutally honest.

In prison, he had thought about her so often that she was as familiar to him as his own wife. More familiar, actually.

He'd relived all the times he'd watched her and interacted with her. He'd liked her on a basic human level. Liked the way she was kind to people. More than once he'd seen her sneak behind Phil's back to sell a customer an antique at a lower price than was marked. He'd seen the way she could make people feel good about themselves with an easy but sincere compliment. He'd been to her house and admired the charming and comfortable home she'd created.

Above and beyond any of that, he'd made her into his ideal sex partner. He'd built on all her good, generous traits and made her into the beautiful woman who would gladly do anything he wanted. When he'd gotten out, he'd told himself that there was no way that the real woman could be as appealing, as sexy, as consuming as the woman he'd created in his mind. Now he couldn't tell if he was seeing her clearly or seeing what he wanted to see. But he did know she'd met Mark Ramsey under rather trying conditions and pretty much kept her cool. He couldn't say the same for himself. All he had to do was hold her hand to get hard. Which was damn inconvenient.

Well, he had an hour to decide whether to meet her at the real estate office. An hour he wasn't going to waste.

He'd fortified himself with lunch at Today's Catch. Now it was time to stop by the Treasure Hunt Pavilion, where a lot of the old crowd would be gathered, although apparently not Molly Dumont. He'd simply assumed she and Phil were running their shop on the premises. Maybe Phil was still there, and maybe they'd split up. That thought gave him a little jolt, and he warned himself to cool it.

The old warehouse was only a few blocks from Shoreside Realty, which would make it easy to get to the appointment—if he decided to keep it.

Back in his car, he headed for the highway, then slowed as he approached the converted processing plant. He'd done an excellent job of the renovation, if he did say so himself. The structure was sound, and he'd blended the restored early twentieth-century details like the ornate molding just under the roofline with modern requirements, such as the handicapped-access walkway that connected the parking lot to the front door.

Again, there was no problem finding a parking space this late in the season, and he wondered which of the dealers had done enough business during the summer to last through the lean winter months.

As he climbed out of the car and stared at the wide front entrance, he felt his chest tighten. He had been proud of his renovation, but he'd never been buddies with the dealers who occupied the interior spaces. They'd represented a tight-knit world of shared experiences that he'd never really been able to enter. Maybe because he'd always secretly thought they'd had something to do with the deterioration of his marriage.

After Veronica had moved into the building, he'd seen her grow closer to the other dealers—and farther away from him.

The tendency to pal around with her colleagues hadn't diminished with time. Veronica had begun staying later and later, going to meetings that lasted far into the evening. And he'd started to suspect that she was having an affair with one of the other shop owners. Veronica had always been a flirt. She'd always attracted guys. He'd known there were a number of the antique dealers who might have crossed the line into sleeping with her.

He'd had several candidates in mind. Like Oliver Garrison and Art Burger. And he'd been reluctantly getting ready to test his theories when her death had changed the whole picture.

Now he stood with his hands in his pockets, thinking it would be amusing to stride into the building as Mike Randall instead of Mark Ramsey. He was equipped to do that, actually. Before he'd had his plastic surgery, he'd taken a trip to Los Angeles and met with one of the top makeup artists in the motion picture industry, Barry Turtledove. Turtledove had made a cast of his face. And from the cast, he'd produced a remarkable mask, just like the kind in the movies where the secret agents were wearing someone else's face. In this case, it was his old face, and it was locked in a carrying case back at the East Point Lodge. He wasn't sure how he was going to use the mask. But once he had a better handle on the prime suspect, he was pretty sure a return visit to Perry's Cove by Mike Randall would be highly useful.

Knowing he was stalling, he walked quickly up the wooden access ramp and through the front door, then stood for a moment, absorbing the atmosphere of the gallery. He could detect an odor he called "old-house smell." Some of the antiques had come from musty old basements or leaky buildings, and they'd carried the scent of their previous surroundings with them. But that was the only negative part of the mix. From where he stood, he could see a pleasing hodgepodge of cabinet pieces, dining-room sets, reupholstered chairs and knickknacks overflowing from curio cabinets and shelves.

The familiar scene sent a wave of nostalgia crashing over him. He'd gotten his appreciation of antiques from his parents, who had been part-time dealers back in New Jersey. In fact, that was how he'd met Veronica. She'd been a regular at the weekend flea markets and antique fairs, too, helping out cousins who were in the business. As teenagers, they'd started hanging out together, and the relationship had gradually changed from friendship to something stronger. He'd thought they were in love, though in retrospect, at eighteen, they'd probably been too young to choose a life's mate. The marriage had been precipitated by Veronica's pregnancy. After they'd gotten hitched, she'd had a miscarriage, and he'd been relieved that he didn't have to support a baby as well as a wife. Apparently Veronica had been relieved, too, because they'd put off having kids—again and again.

Both of them were busy. While he was learning the ropes in the construction business from his uncle, he doggedly took courses at the local community college until he got a degree in business. Veronica was spending time at garage and estate sales, picking up finds she could resell at the flea market and then at the small shop she bought into with her cousins. It had been her idea to move to North Carolina. After eight years of marriage he'd liked the idea of starting over in a new community. And when she'd suggested refurbishing this building and turning it into Treasure Hunt Pavilion, he'd liked that idea, too. She'd even come up with the scheme of getting together a group of dealers to finance the project—which he'd thought of as a stroke of genius at the time.

His musings about the past were cut off abruptly by a familiar voice, low and sharp, coming from his right. It was Oliver Garrison, the largest shareholder and the president of the corporation that managed the enterprise.

From where Mark was standing, his view of the man was blocked by a gallery full of furnishings, including an oversize armoire. But an instant mental picture formed of a man a little over medium height, well muscled from moving large cabinet pieces around, hair just graying at the temples, deep-set eyes that could go from warm to icy in an instant.

Either Garrison was talking on the phone, or he had someone in there with him. He sounded angry now, or upset, but Mark couldn't catch what he was saying.

Would a tourist who had wandered into this place politely stay away from the angry voice? A well-mannered tourist, perhaps. But there were plenty of curious folks around who might be interested enough to approach.

With a mental shrug, Mark stepped past the armoire, then treaded his way through a tastefully arranged seating group and around a marble angel that looked as if it had been stolen from a cemetery.

Garrison wasn't talking on the phone. Another man was with him, his back to Mark. But he stopped short when he recognized the broad shoulders underneath a blue uniform shirt and the buzz-cut hair above the beefy neck.

Lord, of all the people he didn't want to see. It was Sheriff Dean Hammer.

Mark stood without moving. Hammer had been the man who had arrested him and carted him off to the state police in the back of a black-and-white cruiser. Too bad that cruiser hadn't been parked in the public lot now. If he'd seen it, Mark would have picked another day to visit the antique gallery.

Garrison's eyes flashed from his companion to the newcomer, and the other man turned.

"Can I help you?" the antique dealer asked.

Mark's mouth was so dry that he was surprised he could make any words come out. But he managed to say, "There doesn't seem to be anybody around. I was looking for information about one of the tables back there." He gestured vaguely behind him.

"Monday is a slow day," Garrison said. "So, many of the dealers aren't on-site. Perhaps I can help you."

"I don't want to interrupt."

"We were finished with our business," Hammer said. He turned back toward Garrison. "Let me know if you have any other problems."

"I will."

Before the sheriff left, he gave Mark an assessing look. It was difficult for Mark to stand in place under the scrutiny. When the lawman departed, he breathed out some of the air trapped in his lungs. He'd known Hammer was a part of the community and had expected to run into him. In fact, he'd thought about finding an excuse to stop in at the man's office, as a way of controlling their first meeting. But very little was working out the way Mark had thought it would. First Bill Bauder. Now Dean Hammer.

It flashed into his mind that perhaps he was being handed advice from a higher power. *Get out of Perry's Cove before it's too late. Go on with your life somewhere else.*

It seemed he wasn't capable of taking that advice. Partly because he wanted to clear his name and partly because he wanted to make someone pay for what they'd done to him.

"You having some trouble around here?" Mark asked when he and Garrison were alone.

"Why do you want to know?" the dealer asked, a slight edge in his voice.

"I'm thinking of renting a property in town. I don't want to end up picking the wrong community."

"No danger of that. Perry's Cove is about as peaceful a place as they come. But you know how modern life is. There's always something. In this case it was teenagers, using the parking lot for a trysting place. Used condoms on the blacktop don't do much for business."

Mark nodded as if he was agreeing.

"You wanted information on a table?"

"Uh, yeah," Mark answered, remembering his excuse for interrupting the conversation with the sheriff. Leading the way into another dealer's domain, he picked a nice-looking Queen Anne table and chairs.

"The price is right here," Garrison said, displaying a tag taped to one leg.

"Sorry. I didn't see it." The figure was high, so he said he'd have to think about it. After thanking the dealer, he began wandering around the building looking at the various areas.

Garrison was right. There weren't many dealers around, but he did see Ann Layton and Sally Ferguson. Art Burger glanced his way but stayed where he was.

In fact, Ann, who had to be in her fifties now and was still dying her hair red, came bustling up to him when he approached her area near the back of the building.

"Can I help you with anything?" she asked in a chipper voice.

"I'm just looking."

"Oh. Well, let me know if there's anything I can do for you."

He hesitated for a moment, then decided what the hell. "I was here a few years ago, and I remember a dealer named Philip Dumont. Is he still around?"

He could tell from Ann's suddenly distressed expression that he'd asked a loaded question.

"I'm afraid Mr. Dumont passed away."

"Oh, I'm sorry," he answered lamely, coping with his own shock. "He...seemed like he was in good health."

Ann lowered her gaze. "Yes," she murmured.

"When did he die?"

The woman thought for a moment. "About three years ago."

He waited for her to give him more information, but apparently that was all she planned to say. Her silence and the look of distress on her face told him that Phil Dumont hadn't died of natural causes. Had somebody murdered the man? The same person who had murdered Veronica?

Wouldn't that be a coincidence?

ONCE SHE'D FELT as if she'd climbed into the middle class. Now she was barely scraping along, Molly thought as she pulled a clean skirt out of the closet. It had come from a secondhand shop in Newport News, where she went to spend her meager shopping budget.

She'd learned thrift from her parents. Their family had been poor but proud. Dad had been a deliveryman, Mom had worked various retail jobs. They'd given her a loving home, but their horizons had been limited. She'd been in her junior year of college, a scholarship student who had to work nights for living expenses, when she'd met the dashing Phil Dumont. She'd disappointed her parents terribly by quitting school to marry him.

For a while it had seemed as if she and Phil had had it made. She'd loved finding old pieces of furniture, fixing them up and selling them at a profit. She'd loved helping people find just the right antique for their homes. And Phil had loved running the business end of the operation.

Then she'd been back on her own, knowing she'd have a lot better career choices if she'd finished college.

She still intended to do that. But not yet. Not until she could put a little money away.

Satisfied with her appearance, she left the house and headed for the realty office.

In the parking lot she sat for a moment, letting her thoughts turn to Mark Ramsey. She'd deliberately kept her mind off him while she'd changed clothes. Really, she hadn't been sure until she arrived at the building that she was actually going to show up.

With a small shrug, she entered the office, then stopped short as she saw Doris Masters watching her. She'd never been entirely comfortable with the slightly pudgy blonde, but she tried not to show her feelings, since she saw no point in creating animosity in the workplace.

"Larry was looking for you," the other agent said.

"Okay."

"You were inspecting some property for him, weren't you?"

Though it was none of Doris's business, she nodded as she headed toward the boss's private domain in the back.

Larry Iverson was sitting behind his desk, talking on the phone. He looked up, saw her and waved her to a seat, where she cooled her heels for several minutes while he discussed the settlement of a property he'd been anxious to get off the market.

He looked like a beachboy going to fat. With blond hair receding from his forehead and a perpetual tan that had carved deep wrinkles at the corners of his eyes, he was as likely to do business from the poolside of his eight-bedroom beach house as from his office. But apparently he'd waited here for her today.

As soon as he hung up, he looked at her expectantly. "Well?"

"I believe the project is on schedule, although I'm not the perfect person to comment," she said, sticking to the question he'd asked and not the more interesting subject of the recent accident.

Apparently, he already knew what had happened. "I hear there was some trouble down there," he said.

"You mean the bucket of shingles that almost split my head open?" she asked, not really surprised that word had already gotten back to him. Perry's Cove was a small town, and news traveled quickly.

"Yeah." He shifted in his seat. "Sorry it happened."

"It wasn't your fault."

"Still, I don't like my people getting injured on the job. I would have gone myself, but I was tied up here and the client wanted a progress report ASAP." He shifted in his seat again. "I hear some tourist pushed you out of the way."

She nodded. She didn't want to discuss the aftermath of the accident, so she switched to a topic she knew Larry would love. "Yes. We got to talking. He said he was interested in rental property."

"Maybe you can talk up home ownership."

She shrugged, thinking that serving the customer had always been less important to Larry than the bottom line.

Doris had left by the time Molly got back to her desk. She had a bunch of messages to return, but she couldn't concentrate on them. Instead, she pulled the information on some rental property that might interest Mark Ramsey, printed out two copies and left one in a folder on her desk.

As she worked, her mind kept wandering back to the man. He'd knocked her out of the way of the falling bucket of shingles, then he'd landed on top of her, and for a few moments his body had been pressed to hers. She'd had to catch her breath—and not just from the fall.

There was no reason to react to him the way she had. He'd only been on top of her because he'd pushed her out of harm's way and they'd both tumbled to the ground. She'd been breathless and shocked, yet she'd also been turned on by that personal contact. He'd been turned on, too. She'd felt his erection pressing against her leg, and in her disorientation, she'd almost moved against it. Then she'd come back to her senses.

She didn't even know the man. They'd been two strangers meeting under odd and dangerous circumstances. Yet he hadn't felt like a stranger. Not at all. There had been something achingly familiar about him. Before she'd seen his face, she'd been sure she knew him, sure he was someone who had come back to her after a long absence. A romance novel she'd read about a couple who had been lovers in a past life drifted into her mind. There had been a strange familiarity between them, and finally they'd figured out their previous relationship. Could that be true in real life? She made a dismissive sound. It made a good story but it was only fiction.

The whole notion was ridiculous, of course. Still, the impression of familiarity simply wouldn't go away. Or the pull she kept feeling. It had been a long time since she'd responded with such frank sexuality to a man. Not since Philip, actually. After his death, she'd been numb and confused. The numbness had subsided, but there hadn't been anyone in Perry's

Cove who captured her interest. Well, there were a few men she might have responded to, but they were married, and her personal code of ethics didn't include poaching on another woman's husband.

That silent observation sparked a ghost of a thought that she tried to hold on to. But it was gone before she could capture anything solid.

She was still pondering her heated response to a complete stranger when a throat-clearing noise made her look up.

Mark Ramsey himself was standing over her desk, looking down at her as though he knew perfectly well where her mind had been wandering.

She felt her face heat as she struggled for composure, then told herself firmly that he wasn't a mind reader, and there was no way he could figure out where her thoughts had been. Yet something about the way he was looking at her made her fear otherwise. Or perhaps his thoughts were paralleling hers. Unwilling to deal with the implications of that, she began shuffling together papers on her desk.

MARK WATCHED HER, seeing the nervous movements of her hands as she pushed papers into a pile.

Was she hiding something incriminating? Or was she reacting to his frank sexual interest?

He had tried to tamp down that interest, but despite his resolve, it kept rising back up, so to speak.

"We were going to look at some rental properties," he reminded her. "Unless it's not convenient," he added, holding his breath as he waited for her response.

"That's fine," she answered. "I have some listings right here. Just let me get the keys."

He waited while she collected her purse, rounded her desk and disappeared down a short hallway.

She was back several minutes later, looking as if she might have freshened her makeup. He liked the effect. And he liked knowing that she wasn't married anymore.

He felt a small pang as the admission surfaced. Her husband had died, apparently under suspicious or tragic circumstances, and he needed to find out why.

Probably Molly had been through a bad time, and he had no right to take advantage of her loss. But he couldn't turn off the secret feeling of elation.

She was free, and he could ask her out—if that was what he wanted to do.

To be frank, what he really wanted to do was make wild, passionate love with her. What would she think if she knew that?

"All set?" he asked.

"Yes."

"Your car or mine?"

"It's probably easier for me to drive. I know my way around here, and you don't," she said.

"Right," he agreed, thinking that she'd saved him from flubbing up. The truth was, he did know his way around the area, and he might well have given that knowledge away if he'd been the one at the wheel.

Her car was a five-year-old Honda. Not a luxury vehicle by any means, but she kept it spotless inside and out.

He climbed into the passenger seat, enjoying the close-up view of her breasts as she shifted into reverse and turned the wheel to exit the parking space.

He was turning into a dirty old man, he thought. The price of his enforced exile from the fair sex.

He pulled his gaze away from Molly's breasts and leaned back into the contour seat, closing his eyes. Still, he was aware of her delicate scent—a combination of soap and flowers and woman. Knowing it could drive him crazy if he let it, he made an attempt to ignore the enticement and focused on the view out the window. "Where are we going?" he asked.

"I've got several properties in mind. One's a beach house."

"Those monstrosities springing up on the sand dunes?"

"Something more suitable to one occupant. And if you don't like that, I can show you a new apartment complex about ten miles from here. The grounds are beautifully landscaped. The units are well equipped, and there's a pool and Jacuzzi."

He didn't think that was what he was looking for, but he didn't voice the objection. The longer it took to find a place, the more excuse he'd have to be with Ms. Dumont.

"So, how did you get into the real estate business?" he asked.

She hesitated for a moment, then answered, "After my husband died, I needed a way to support myself. We'd been antique dealers and I'd always been good with people, so a friend suggested I try real estate. Larry Iverson took me on as an office assistant while I was taking classes to get my license."

He nodded, wishing she'd said a little more about her husband. Apparently it wasn't a subject she wanted to explore with one of her clients.

Their first stop was a small house across the highway from the beach. The place was in good shape, had an excellent view of the old lighthouse and was well laid out, but he knew as soon as he saw it that he wasn't going to live in it. The last time he'd been here was for a party given by one of the antique dealers. He and Veronica had been in the midst of a fight, and they'd avoided each other all evening.

Since he couldn't explain any of that to Molly, he let her show him around, then found reasons he didn't like the interior.

She didn't press him to rent the place, only suggested that they move on to another property.

Five miles down the highway, she turned in at an artificially weathered signboard announcing the community of Ocean Vista. The access road led to a development of three-story buildings, each with a sheltered balcony. The landscaping was lush, with a foundation of small shrubs and beds of carefully tended annuals.

There hadn't been any complexes like this when he'd lived in Perry's Cove, but land must be getting scarce now, making group housing more attractive to both developers and buyers.

''Is this place open for residency?'' he asked, peering around at the almost empty parking lot and the new buildings.

''Barely. Most of the units are still up for sale. This one was bought by a man who wants to rent it out for a few years before retiring down here.''

She led him up an outside stairway to a rectangular landing, where the doors were painted in sun-drenched yellows and jungle greens.

As he followed her inside, he was vaguely surprised that the rooms were already furnished, in casual wicker with sessile rugs on the tile floors. The kitchen was small but adequate for his needs. He'd never been a gourmet cook, and he hadn't picked up any culinary skills working in the prison library.

He noted that the appliances weren't top of the line.

Molly pointed out the virtues of the condo as she led him down the hall to the bedroom and then the bathroom, which followed the modern-luxury trend to large and bright, with a spa tub and a separate shower.

He'd been keeping his mind on business, but as he eyed the room, he couldn't cancel a sudden image of himself and Molly standing together in the shower, water cascading over their naked bodies.

The picture was so vivid that he drew in a sharp breath and reached out and grabbed the doorjamb to steady himself.

"Are you all right?" she asked.

"Yeah," he managed to say. "I guess the altitude is getting to me."

"The altitude? We're at sea level."

He laughed. "Well, something's getting to me. Maybe I'm allergic to the place."

"Then we should leave."

He followed her back through the condo, then waited while she locked the door.

"Do you want to see some of the grounds?" she asked.

"Yes," he answered, not because he was interested in the scenery but because getting back into the car would mean getting close to her again, and he was pretty sure that was a bad idea.

He was still feeling out of kilter as they started down a gravel pathway that led along the side of the building, his attention focused on the vinyl siding of the closest apartment.

He stopped, his gaze drawn to a place where a rust

stain was already starting to bleed from the balcony railing onto the wall. He was thinking that the builder had used shoddy materials, then decided that was none of his business since he wasn't planning to take the apartment. Looking up, he noticed that Molly was ten yards ahead of him, marching purposefully along the path, her heels clicking against the gravel chips.

She had almost reached a section of the walkway that was covered with a three-by-three piece of plywood. The wood wasn't squarely over the sidewalk, but set at a slight angle as though someone had tossed it carelessly onto the ground.

His eyes went from her to the plywood, and in the back of his mind he was thinking that walking around it would be a good idea—except that there was no place else to tread besides the recently planted landscaping.

"Wait!" he called, quickening his pace. But she already had one foot poised above the flat surface. He heard a splintering sound as her foot came down on the wood.

Chapter Four

Even as Mark started running forward, he watched the plywood crack, watched Molly sway unsteadily on her feet. This time he was too far away to save her, and he saw her tumbling to the side.

He pictured her leg going through the surface and her skin being torn by the jagged splinters.

But she avoided the worst of the damage by grabbing hold of a small, ornamental tree that had been planted along the pathway.

The poor, abused sapling swayed under the unaccustomed weight but stayed in the ground, while the plywood went shooting in the opposite direction, taking Molly's shoe with it.

Some tiny portion of his brain noted that the wood had been covering an underground service panel, now gaping open. The information barely registered because almost all of his attention was focused on Molly as she struggled to stay erect.

He reached her and gathered her in his arms, detaching her from the tree trunk, so that she had something more secure to cling to—himself. She transferred her grip to his waist and shoulders, her hands clamping on to him with a kind of fierce desperation.

He knew the emergency hardly matched the incident with the bucket of shingles. But perhaps they were both reacting to the repetition of events. Twice in one day someone had put Molly in danger, and once again he had charged forward to the rescue.

And once again, as he clasped her in his embrace, he was swamped by sensations. The feel of her slender body. The brush of her soft hair against his cheek. The sweet woman scent that had driven him crazy in the car. Perhaps that scent was what drew him most deeply—after all the deprivations of prison life, or perhaps it was the way Molly clung to him, as though he was her savior, although he hadn't done much. He'd been too far away to be of any real help. This time she'd saved herself from injury by her quick reaction.

Undoubtedly she could stand on her own now, but still she held on to him. For long moments, her gaze was directed downward as if she was debating what to do next.

He held his breath, waiting. Slowly, slowly she raised her face, meeting his questioning gaze.

There was only a brief moment of eye contact, but it was enough for important messages to be exchanged.

He silently asked if she wanted him to turn her loose. She told him she wanted to stay where she was.

And with that unspoken agreement, it was the most natural thing in the world for him to lower his lips to hers.

Images of kissing her, touching her had saved his sanity when he'd been locked away from the world. And now here she was in his arms, telling him she wanted the same thing he did.

The meeting of their lips was like lightning striking

dry tinder in some dark, primeval forest. There was nothing slow and deliberate about the contact. The moment his mouth settled on hers, the kiss flared white-hot, swamping his senses. She tasted better than fine wine, better than freedom, better than all the things he had thought he could never have again.

He drank from her like a man deprived of all sustenance and finally bidden to partake of a feast.

She seemed just as greedy as her mouth opened, worked against his, sending searing signals to all of his nerve endings.

He was instantly hard as granite, instantly ready to make love with her. His only thought was to satisfy his own desperate need for intimate contact. One hand slid down to her hips, pulling her against his erection, while the other hand pressed against her back, bringing her breasts against his chest.

His mind spun out of control. He needed Molly, needed to be deep inside her. His hand stroked her hips, over the rounded curve of her bottom. He broke the kiss and lifted his head, his eyes barely focused as he searched for a place where the two of them could make love.

Her indrawn breath brought his gaze back to her face, and the dazed yet alarmed look in her eyes was like a dash of cold water.

He blinked. What was he doing—planning to ravage her out here in the shrubbery?

He'd known that years of deprivation had made him needy, but he hadn't realized he would turn into a raving maniac when he took Molly Dumont into his arms.

His heart was slamming against the wall of his chest, his breath uneven and jagged.

He forced himself to loosen his hold on her and take a step back, although he kept one hand on her arm, because he couldn't bear to break the contact completely.

"I'm sorry," he managed to say, his voice thick, as he stared into her flushed face. "I think I came on a little too strong."

Lord, she looked so beautiful with her skin rosy and her lips reddened from the kiss. He wanted to pull her back into his arms, but he ordered himself to keep his free hand against his side.

She answered his apology with a tight nod, and he knew he had to come up with a lot more than sorry if he ever wanted her in his arms again.

The sudden sense of loss stole his breath away. He dragged shaky fingers through his hair as he fumbled for the right words. "I...I haven't been with a woman since my wife died," he heard himself explaining.

"Oh. I'm sorry. I mean about your wife."

She took several moments before asking, "How long?"

"Too long." He didn't want to lie. Not to Molly. And he didn't want to get specific—not when the time frame would put him back at the scene of the crime. Instead he brought the conversation back to her. "Are you okay?"

"Yes," she answered, and he felt as if the response had been automatic.

"Did you hurt your foot?"

She looked down at her shoeless toes, visible through her stocking, and he was sure she'd forgotten all about the piece of plywood. Then her eyes darted to the section of path that had been covered up. When she saw the hole in the ground where the service panel should have been, she made a sharp, surprised sound.

"You could have gotten badly hurt," he muttered. "You did some quick thinking."

"I felt the wood give and I pulled back. It was just instinct."

He started to continue the discussion, then stopped abruptly. He wanted to know if she'd been specifically targeted both now and at the Calico Duck. But they were in the middle of the condo complex, and he couldn't be sure that they wouldn't be overheard. Of course, he hadn't considered their lack of privacy when he'd been about to throw her into a flower bed and plunge himself into her, he thought with a grimace.

"What?" she asked as she caught his facial expression.

"Maybe we should cool off with a walk on the beach."

Seconds passed as she mulled that idea over, and he thought she was going to refuse before she said, "Okay."

He let out the breath he'd been holding. Then he walked around the hole in the path, being careful not to crush the new plantings. When he reached the piece of plywood, he squatted and worked the heel of her shoe out of the wood. Holding it up for inspection, he saw there was a long gash in the leather.

"Can you get it fixed?" he asked as he handed the shoe over.

"Maybe."

As Molly slipped the shoe back on, he picked up the plywood and looked at the place where her heel had broken through. "Whoever put this here is an idiot. The wood is too damn thin to cover a hole in the path.''

He started along the side of the building, this time taking the lead as he kept his eyes trained on the ground. There appeared to be no more booby traps.

They rounded the corner of a condo and emerged onto a natural area where sea oats waved in the wind blowing off the ocean. He sat down on one of the new benches that had been placed at intervals along the edge of the complex and took off his shoes and socks.

Molly turned away from him and fumbled with her skirt. When he saw that she was taking off her torn panty hose, he averted his eyes. Not out of chivalry, exactly. He knew that if he watched her, he was going to want her again.

Hell, just thinking about her peeling the clinging nylon down her legs was making him hard. He was in a bad way.

With a grimace, he stood up and stepped onto the sand, lifting his face to the wind from the ocean, hoping to cool his overheated skin.

He'd taken only five or six steps before his foot came down on a buried piece of two-by-four.

``Damn!''

``What?''

He bent and dug up the piece of wood. ``Another booby trap. Whoever built this place needs to clean up their beach.''

``I'll send in complaints.''

They both watched where they were walking now as they crossed the sand toward the waves ebbing and flowing along the shoreline.

The noise of the ocean covered their conversation as he asked, ``So who knew you were coming here?''

"Nobody."

"You're sure about that?"

She considered her answer. "Well, I guess somebody could have checked my log. I keep a record of where I'm taking clients. Just in case."

"In case of what?"

"In case I get into trouble, if you really want to know. Real estate isn't the safest job in the world. You're going into vacant properties with men you barely know."

"I wouldn't hurt you," he said quickly.

"I'm not so sure."

The accusation stung. "Now wait a minute."

"I don't mean you'd assault me physically," she clarified. "I mean, are you planning to stay in Perry's Cove?"

"I don't know."

"Well, then, when you leave, I could get hurt."

She was being up front with him. He swallowed, thinking he didn't have that option. From her point of view, they barely knew each other, yet he'd kissed her as though he were a prisoner of war finally coming home to his beloved.

The analogy was too close for comfort. And dangerous, as well. He wanted Molly sexually, but making an emotional commitment would be pretty rash.

"Let's go back to the accident. I mean the one involving the plywood," he said. "That's two in one day."

"Are you trying to say somebody is going after me?"

He shrugged.

"I say it's a terrible coincidence!" She shifted her

gaze away from him, facing the waves rolling and crashing on the sand.

The tide was coming in, and the low edge of foam swept toward them. Neither one of them moved, and the water swirled around their feet, bringing a burst of deep, stinging cold.

Ignoring Molly's denial, he continued with his line of questioning. "Have you gotten into a fight with anyone, angered anyone?"

"Not that I know of," she answered, but he picked up a note of uncertainty in her voice.

"Okay."

"You sound like you don't believe me."

He shrugged. "Something's happening here."

"Well, if someone was out to get me, they would have had to go into the office after I left, then rush out to this property before we arrived and set up that piece of plywood."

"You had this place listed second in your log?"

"Yes," she answered reluctantly, "but so what? If someone wanted to hurt me, they wouldn't know that we were going to take that path through the complex. It wasn't like what happened this morning, where I was in a much more confined area."

He nodded, hoping she was right.

"How did your husband die?" he suddenly asked.

He saw her face go pale. "That's none of your business."

"What if someone came after him and now they're coming after you?"

"He shot himself. Nobody came after him."

He was stunned by the information—and instantly contrite. Now it was his turn to say, "I'm sorry. I mean, I'm sorry about the way it happened.'' He hesitated a moment before asking, ''Why did he do it?''

She moistened her lips. ''Like I told you, we used to have an antique business. As far as I could tell, we were doing okay. But he was the one who took care of the finances. I was the one who artistically arranged the merchandise and interacted with the customers.''

He nodded, thinking that her description of the division of duties was what he remembered.

''I assumed we were solvent. It turned out all the money had evaporated.'' She stopped and made a small huffing sound before going on. ''I keep wondering now if he had some secret life that I never knew about. Like maybe he was a compulsive gambler and managed to hide that fault from me.''

''That sounds...frustrating.''

''It was.'' She waited a beat before asking, ''What about your wife?''

''I'm not ready to talk about her.''

''Oh.''

He scuffed his bare foot against the sand, thinking that he'd trapped himself. He'd wanted to know about Phil, but he couldn't talk about Veronica. Not yet, certainly. And he didn't want to make up a lie. ''Maybe when I know you better,'' he offered.

''We should go on to the next place,'' she said, her voice a little remote. He was pretty sure she was hurt by his refusal to share the same kind of information she'd given him.

He nodded, turning quickly back toward the condo complex. Movement in the shadows drew his eye. Someone was watching them, someone who ducked around the corner when he saw he'd been spotted.

Another coincidence? Someone just curious about

the couple on the beach? Maybe, but Mark didn't think so. He was damn well going to find out who was interested in Molly and himself. He took off across the stretch of beach, running as fast as he could in the dry, shifting sand. He almost made it to the landscaping along the edge of the complex when another hidden hazard tripped him up. Pain shot through his bare toes where they'd connected with something hard, and he had to work to keep his balance.

With a curse, he tried to find his stride again, but the pain slowed him down as he darted into the pathway where he and Molly had earlier emerged.

By the time he reached the parking lot, a car was rapidly backing out of a space. He ran forward, trying to read the license plate, but it was smeared with mud. All he saw was a silver Honda speeding away.

Breathing raggedly, he brushed the sand off his pant legs, then sat down hard on a set of steps. When another flash of movement caught his attention, he looked up, prepared to defend himself. It was Molly, coming around the corner of the building, carrying both their pairs of shoes and her panty hose.

"What was that?" she asked, her eyes darting from him to the parking lot.

"A spy."

He saw her face go pale. "What do you mean, a spy?"

"Someone who was interested in what we were doing here and who took off when I spotted him. Do you know anyone who owns a silver Honda?"

She shrugged. "Not that I know of, but I don't pay a lot of attention to cars."

"Too bad."

"I'm sorry."

"I'm not blaming it on you."

He shifted his foot and winced when his toes barely touched the concrete.

"You're hurt," she observed.

"It's nothing."

"That's what all the macho guys say. Let's have a look." She knelt in front of him and picked up his foot, cradling it in her palm.

Despite the circumstances, the touch felt intimate. He leaned back and closed his eyes, sprawling across the steps, allowing himself to enjoy the sensation of her fingers sliding over his skin.

"Am I hurting you?" she asked.

"No." He heard the strangled quality of his voice as he lay there unable to move.

He was jolted back to reality when her finger slid across the end of his big toe. "That hurts."

"The skin isn't broken. But I think you're going to have a bruise. I can go back inside and get you some ice."

"I'll be okay. Let's just get out of here." Sitting up, he reached for his shoes and socks. After gingerly slipping on the socks, he went on to the shoes, glad that the pair weren't too tight.

They got back into the car, and Molly inserted the key in the ignition, then sat staring through the windshield.

"Why would someone be interested in what we're doing?" she asked.

"I don't know," he answered, wondering if it was possible that somebody had caught on to him already. Denial came on the heels of the question, yet he couldn't entirely dismiss the nagging doubt.

"Do you want to call it quits for the day?" Molly asked.

"No. Let's look at some more properties," he said aloud. Inwardly he was thinking he might have another chance to find out who was following them around—if anybody *was* following them.

They were both silent as she turned onto the highway. They were heading toward his old house, and he found his chest tightening as his eyes scanned the mailboxes. He'd come into town from the other direction, and he hadn't been up this way yet.

The yellow and red For Sale sign at the end of the driveway was like a jolt to his senses. "There's a real estate sign," he heard himself saying when he knew he should keep his mouth shut.

"That's not a rental property."

"I'd like to see it," he insisted.

"A woman was murdered in that house."

He felt as if she'd punched him in the gut, and struggled to keep breathing normally. Had Veronica been murdered there? He didn't know. How could Molly have more information than he did? He shot her a quick glance. She looked nervous, but she would if she thought this had really been a murder site. He craned his neck, just barely able to see the roofline from where they sat.

"In that house? Are you sure?" he asked.

She shook her head. "I guess I shouldn't have put it that way. The woman of the house was murdered, and her husband was convicted. Then new evidence came to light, and he got out of prison."

"I guess that makes the place hard to sell."

"Yes."

"Maybe I can get a good deal on it," he said. "Let's go have a look."

She made a small sound but did as he asked, turning in at the driveway. The road had seen better days, and she drove slowly to avoid the ruts.

"What was her name?" he asked.

"Veronica Randall."

He let the name hang in the closed atmosphere of the car. "I think I heard about the case," he finally said. "I felt sorry for the poor guy. I guess somebody set him up."

"That's what I always thought."

He felt some of the tightness in his chest ease, until he reminded himself that she could just be making conversation. Or maybe now that Mike Randall had gained his freedom, she was voicing the safer opinion.

"Who would have wanted to make it look like he murdered his wife?" he asked.

She shrugged, and he turned toward her, watching the way her hands gripped the wheel and the deep look of concentration on her face as she negotiated the rutted lane. Was the driving really all that difficult, or was she glad of the excuse to keep her attention focused on the task?

He stopped wondering about her as they crested a small rise and the house came into view. Breathing was almost impossible as he stared at the Cape Cod he'd called home for five years. About the same amount of time he'd been in prison, actually. Memories assaulted him, some good, some terrible. He and Veronica had bought the place as a fixer-upper, and he'd put in hours of sweat equity, making it comfortable, weather tight and structurally sound. When Veronica had asked him to blast the ugly black paint off the fireplace and restore it to natural brick, he'd been glad to tackle the difficult task. She was the one who had done the decorating, mostly with wonderful finds she'd brought home from flea markets or traded from other dealers at antique shows.

He'd been proud of their home, and at first they'd been happy. Then, little by little, their life together had begun disintegrating. He wasn't even sure when it started happening. He'd been busy with his construction company, and maybe that was part of the problem. Maybe he hadn't paid enough attention to her. All he knew was that one day he'd realized that they were both miserable.

While his mind had been stuck in the past, he'd silently gotten out of the car and walked toward the front door, thinking that the house needed painting. One of the shutters was hanging at a drunken angle.

Molly's voice brought him back to the present. "We can't go in."

"Why not?"

"Because...I don't have the key."

He didn't even miss a beat. "People hide keys outside."

"We're talking about a house that hasn't been lived in in six years."

"Let me look anyway," he said, starting to search through the bushes. He knew where he'd always hidden the key. Either it was there or not. He quickly spotted the fake rock, but he didn't go right to it. Instead, he pretended to extend his search, all the while aware that Molly's speculative gaze was fixed on him.

Maybe this wasn't such a good idea, a tiny voice in his head warned. Maybe he should get out while the getting was good. But he was in the grip of a compulsion that was making his heart pound and his palms turn sticky.

Unable to wait any longer, he went back and picked up the rock. "Found it!"

She looked around uneasily. "Mark, this isn't such a good idea," she said, echoing his earlier thought.

He didn't listen to either one of them. Instead, he hurried to the front door and inserted the key.

The moment the door swung open, he knew he had made a mistake.

Chapter Five

He got only a quick glance into the living room. It was bare, except for the dried reddish-brown substance splattered about in a random pattern. The smell told him it wasn't ketchup.

He backed out of the house, slamming the door behind him, silently cursing his impulsive decision to come here. If Molly weren't with him, he would have gotten back into the car and driven away at top speed. But that wasn't an option now.

Behind him, her voice unsteady, she broke into his frantic thoughts. ''What's wrong?''

''Blood,'' he muttered.

''Oh, God. No.'' Her face contorted. ''Let's get out of here.''

He couldn't hide his shock. She was having the same response as he was, and he needed to understand why. Before he could form a question, a cloud of sand appeared over the rise, and another car came roaring up the lane like Old Nick was behind it.

When it pulled to a stop in front of them and he saw the short, balding man who climbed out, Mark knew that he was well and truly trapped. There was no way to get out of the mess he'd created besides owning up to what he'd just found. Silently, he reached back and rubbed his fingers over the place where he'd gripped the doorknob, hoping he was smearing his prints enough to make them untraceable—although he supposed it wasn't outside the realm of possibility that Mike Randall's prints were still on the doorknob. Did fingerprints age? He wished he'd checked up on that detail.

Molly interrupted his whirling thoughts. "It's Bill Bauder," she whispered. "The newspaper editor. He sticks his nose into everything around here."

As Bauder approached them, an image flashed in his mind, an image of himself running headlong down the beach. He managed to stand where he was by reminding himself that the editor didn't have a clue who he was.

"What's going on here?" Bauder asked.

"Ms. Dumont was showing me this house," Mark answered, keeping his voice low and controlled.

"You're the guy who said you were interested in rental property?"

"Yes. How do you know?"

"It's my business to know what's going on in Perry's Cove," Bauder answered before pointing out the obvious. "This place isn't for rent."

Mark slipped his hands into his pockets. "Ms. Dumont was giving me some local history. When she told me the house was connected with a murder, I couldn't resist having a look at it." He turned to Molly. "How long ago was it?"

"Six years. Something like that," she murmured.

"Unfortunately, when I stepped inside, I saw what looked like blood. That's why we're standing out here."

The man's eyes widened. "Blood?"

"Right, but I assume somebody would have cleaned it up from six years ago."

Bauder looked at him appraisingly. "And how did you get inside?"

Mark flicked Molly a quick glance, then made a hasty decision. "The door was unlocked."

Beside him, he saw Molly shift her weight from one foot to the other. They both knew he'd gone looking for the key. Now he didn't want to admit that. It sounded too calculating. His breath turned shallow as he waited for her to correct his version of the events. Instead, she nodded, and he felt some of the tightness in his chest ease.

Bauder strode to the door, gripped the knob and turned it. More fingerprints obscuring his own, Mark thought.

"Thanks," he murmured in a voice so low that only Molly could catch the words.

She looked as if she wanted to answer him, but they didn't really have any privacy, not when Bauder stopped in his tracks almost as soon as he'd stepped briskly inside.

"Damn," the editor muttered as he rejoined them in the front yard. "What happened in there?"

Mark spread his hands. "Your guess is as good as ours. Probably someone should call the sheriff," he said, keeping his voice even. He and Molly had both been prepared to leave the scene of the crime until they'd been trapped here. Now he was acting helpful.

"I can make the call for you," Bauder said, whipping out his cell phone. It wasn't 911, Mark realized as soon as he heard the conversation. Apparently the editor had the sheriff's private line.

"Dean, there's a problem at the Randall house," Bauder said with no preamble.

Dean, Mark thought. Pretty chummy.

In response to a question, the editor continued, "Molly Dumont was showing a client the property, and it looks like there's been a massacre inside."

"I wouldn't call it a massacre," Mark said under his breath. There had been blood, but he hadn't seen any body parts. He didn't have any idea what had happened in there. Neither did Bauder, unless he had been personally involved and had been lying in wait, hoping someone would stumble onto the mess he'd created.

Even as those thoughts formed, Mark recognized them as paranoid. Probably Bauder was simply exercising his newsman's flare for the dramatic.

He clicked off and turned back to Mark. "The sheriff will be here momentarily. He'd like to talk to you."

"We haven't done anything wrong," Mark answered, knowing as he said the words that they were absolutely no protection.

He hadn't done anything wrong six years ago, and he'd ended up in prison. The old memories had the power to make his palms go damp and his heart start to race.

Struggling to shift his thoughts away from himself, he slid Molly a quick glance and saw that she was standing rigidly beside him like a soldier facing a firing squad.

As soon as he took in her reaction, he wanted to sling a protective arm around her shoulder, but Bauder was watching them closely and Mark wasn't going to do anything that might look inappropriate for their supposed relationship. As far as anyone else knew—

as far as Molly knew—they had just met a few hours ago. He didn't want to read in the local paper that the widow Molly Dumont seemed very cozy with a new client.

He'd given himself an excellent reason for not touching her. But it wasn't the only one. He'd had lots of practice in prison keeping his expression neutral, but he knew the poker face would dissolve if he made physical contact with her. So he stayed where he was.

"You just got here?" Bauder asked casually. But Mark wasn't fooled. He'd heard that voice turn from neutral to accusatory in the blink of an eye.

He'd never liked Bill Bauder. He'd never trusted the man, even before the *Voice of Perry's Cove* had taken up the vendetta against him. He knew that showing weakness in front of the editor was a mistake, so instead of shifting his gaze away, he gave the man a direct look. "I think you must know that we just arrived," he answered, "since you showed up minutes after we did. Were you following us or something? I mean, is every real estate transaction down here a news story?"

The editor had the grace to look embarrassed. "I wasn't following you. I have my sources of information," he said. "The Randall house is news. Someone saw a car turn in here, and I was in the vicinity."

"Well, I pity the poor bastard who buys this place," he answered, then decided it was better not to establish his new persona as a belligerent character, so he switched his tone from confrontational to casual.

"So what can you tell me about the old case?" he asked.

"The husband, Mike Randall, was convicted of his

wife's murder. Then he hired a slick lawyer from up north who got the conviction reversed."

"So you think he really was guilty and his lawyer got him off?" Mark pressed.

"I'm still reserving judgment."

Sure, Mark thought. DNA evidence was just a crock of moonshine. There had been plenty of inflammatory stories in the paper six years ago when Mike Randall had been accused of murder. Had Bauder written anything about the conviction being reversed, or wasn't that important enough to print?

He might have followed that line of inquiry, but a new sand cloud announced the arrival of another vehicle.

Show time.

AS MOLLY WATCHED the black-and-white cruiser coming over the curve of the hill, her stomach clenched. She had good reasons to despise Dean Hammer. But she wasn't going to let the sheriff see anything of what she was feeling. Like Bill Bauder, he was an expert at seizing on weakness and twisting it to his advantage.

She cut a glance toward the man at her side. From the way he was standing, it looked as if he wasn't any more pleased about confronting the law than she was.

He'd lied about how they'd gotten into the house and she wanted to know why. Just the way he was probably wondering why she'd wanted to cut and run as soon as he'd found the mess inside.

But there was no way they were going to exchange any of that information until they were alone again.

The police car pulled to a stop and Hammer climbed out in that officious way he had, stopping to adjust the belt that held his gun and all the other equipment that made him look like a walking arsenal. He had a deputy with him. A guy named Cory Daniels, whom Molly didn't like, either.

The sheriff nodded to his friend Bauder, then waited until he was three feet from Mark and herself before saying in his lazy drawl, "I hear there's been a deal of trouble up here."

"It looks that way," Mark answered, "but I can't tell for sure what happened."

"And you would be...?" the sheriff asked, getting out a notepad and pen.

"Mark Ramsey," he answered, his voice steady.

"I saw you earlier. At the antique mall."

"That's right."

Molly looked at Mark. Before he'd thrown her to the ground at the Calico Duck or after? Somehow the mall was the last place she would have pictured him going.

"What's your business in town?" the sheriff asked. Beside him, his deputy remained silent. But Molly couldn't stop herself from calculating the odds. Three against two.

"I'm a writer," he said, giving the same answer he'd given her.

"And how did you end up here? I mean, at this particular location?" The lawman gestured toward the house.

"When Ms. Dumont told me there had been a murder connected with this property, I wanted to see it. I guess I should have left well enough alone."

Hammer didn't agree or disagree. "When did you arrive in town?" he asked.

Molly noted the even tone of Mark's voice as he

answered. "Last night. I checked into the East Point Lodge. Today I went looking for a place to eat. Which is how I happened to meet up with Ms. Dumont."

She listened with interest to his low-key account of their dramatic first encounter.

All eyes shot to her. "You didn't report any accident," the deputy said, speaking for the first time.

"I went home and cleaned up. Then I went to the office and reported the incident to my boss, since I'd agreed to meet Mr. Ramsey there. Didn't Larry call you?"

"No," Hammer snapped.

It was a small relief when the law officer asked them to wait while he and his deputy went inside the house. Their inspection was almost as brief as Mark's and Bauder's had been. Stepping outside again, Hammer clicked on his cell phone, and she could hear him requesting a crime scene investigation team from the state crime lab.

Her attention was focused on the sheriff, when a flash of light made her blink, and she looked up to see Bauder standing with a camera pointed at them.

"Hey, what are you doing?" she asked.

"Reporting the news."

"You don't have permission to use my photo."

"This isn't a feature article. It's a news story. I don't need your permission."

She sighed, figuring that was probably right given the way embarrassed townspeople regularly ended up in the pages of the *Voice of Perry's Cove*. She'd played that role herself, three years ago, after Phil had died. They both had, actually. There had been photos of herself looking distraught and also photos showing Molly and Phil Dumont in happier times.

Her attention was snapped back to the present by a sarcastically delivered question from the newspaper editor. "What were you thinking coming up here?"

Before she could dredge up an answer, Mark jumped in. "Isn't it pretty obvious? She's a real estate agent, and she was accommodating a client."

Grateful for the show of support, she turned to him. He looked as if he wanted to close the distance between them and pull her close, or was she just projecting her own needs onto him?

At any rate, he stayed where he was, for reasons she could understand very well. If Bill Bauder caught a hint of anything personal between them, he'd want to know why. And that wasn't a question she could honestly answer, since she'd ended up in a passionate embrace with a man she barely knew.

She tuned back in on the conversation.

"So don't put this on her," Mark was saying. "I want it on the record, when you write about this incident, that I made the request to see this house."

"Will do," Bauder retorted. Then, "You should have curbed your curiosity."

"Hindsight is always sharp," Mark muttered. "We were talking about a murder that happened years ago. If I'd thought there was something wrong now, I certainly wouldn't have suggested we come here."

Molly noted the body language of the two men. It was obvious that they had taken an instant dislike to each other.

Dean Hammer ambled toward them again. She'd never thought the sheriff would be a welcome intrusion in her life, but it was a relief when he turned to Mark and asked, "You say you're at the East Point Lodge?"

"Yes. I was planning to stay there until I found a place of my own. Now I'm wondering if this town has the atmosphere I was looking for."

That observation sent a stab of disappointment shooting through her. Was Mark really leaving town so soon, or was he just making a point? She added that to her list of questions.

"I'd appreciate it if you hung around until we clear this up," Hammer said, sounding more like he was issuing an order rather than making a request. For good measure, he added, "You'd best be getting back to your house-hunting now. This is a crime scene and off limits to the public."

His parting shot to Molly was, "And you'd best stick to your planned itinerary."

While she was murmuring her agreement, Mark jumped in with a comment similar to his earlier statement to Bauder. "I want to make it clear that she deviated from her planned itinerary because I asked her to accommodate me."

Probably he was feeling guilty about dragging her into the middle of this mess.

"Noted," the sheriff answered.

It looked as if Mark might come back with another retort, a bad idea where Dean Hammer was concerned, so she gently put her hand on his arm. "We really better be going."

His gaze flicked to her, and he nodded.

"If you have any information for me, here's my number," the sheriff said, fishing in his pocket and handing Mark a white business card.

He pocketed the card, then escorted her back to the car and held the driver's door open while she slipped behind the wheel.

Neither one of them spoke as she backed around to face down the long driveway and headed away from the house. It was as if they were both thinking that the sheriff or Bauder might whip out a directional mike and listen in on their conversation.

At the end of the driveway, she stopped and turned to him. "Thanks for sticking up for me."

"I'm the one who got us into trouble," he answered.

"You didn't know what was going to happen."

"Nevertheless." He waited a beat, then said, "Thanks for backing me up when I told Bauder the door was unlocked. I decided it wouldn't look great if I admitted searching for the key."

"I understand." She turned her head toward him. "Your instincts are good, by the way."

"You don't mean my opening the door."

"No. About wanting to clear out before we were detected." She dragged in a breath and let it out in a rush. "Probably you're wondering why I wanted to leave and pretend that we'd never been here."

"Yeah, that was a question in my mind."

She sucked in a breath and let it out slowly. "When Hammer gets his teeth into something, he won't let it go. After my husband, Phil, died, Hammer acted like his death was part of some big conspiracy. He asked me questions that were none of his business. And when I couldn't answer them the way he wanted, he asked them again and again. I'm not sure what he was trying to prove. I ended up feeling like he thought I had something to do with Phil's death."

"I'm sorry."

"I've avoided him ever since. So I didn't like seeing that police car come up the driveway."

"I understand," Mark answered, and she had the feeling it wasn't simply an automatic response.

Figuring she had nothing to lose, she asked, "What was your brush with the law?"

He looked startled. "What makes you think I had a brush with the law?"

"Your reaction when Hammer got out of the car and came toward us. I could tell you were uptight."

"It was a long time ago," he answered but said no more.

When the silence stretched, she clarified, "And you're not going to tell me about it."

"That's right."

"So I get to keep revealing things about myself, and you get to keep ducking my questions."

"I'm sorry. I'm a private person."

"Sometimes it helps to talk about the bad stuff," she said, giving him another chance to put their relationship on an even footing. She wanted to like Mark Ramsey. She'd certainly responded to him in a way she hadn't to any other man since Phil.

Well, to be honest, there had been one other man. Mike Randall. She'd been attracted to him but hadn't done anything about that attraction. Not when her husband was alive.

There was something about Mark that reminded her of Mike. In those first instants after the bucket of shingles had fallen off the roof, when he'd been lying on top of her, she'd thought it was Mike come back. Despite the circumstances, she'd felt a spurt of gladness. Then she'd seen his face, and she'd known she was mistaken.

Now she waited with her chest growing painfully tight—waited for him to share his background with her. She'd covered for him when he'd made up that story about the door being unlocked and she'd felt a kind of alliance forming between them when they'd faced Bauder and then Hammer.

Finally, when his silence stretched to breaking point, she forced herself to say, "This doesn't seem to be working out."

"What do you mean?" he asked.

"I mean, it looks like we haven't built up a bond of trust. I think it would be better if you found a different real estate agent."

She saw him swallow. "Does it take a bond of trust to move rental property?"

"No. But I think you understand what I'm talking about. You're not stupid, just...closed up. And..."

"And what?" he demanded sharply.

"And you're hiding something."

He gave a small nod of acknowledgment, and she felt her hope rising again. But the silence between them only seemed to thicken. Instead of what she wanted to hear, he said, "I'll leave my cell phone number with you, in case you change your mind."

She reined in her disappointment. Somehow she'd been hoping that her stance would tip the balance, but apparently that was just wishful thinking.

The pen felt like lead in her hand as she took down the number. Then, resolutely, she drove him back to the real estate office. They didn't speak again, and when she pulled to a stop in front of the small building, he climbed out and walked toward his car. A deep feeling of loss gripped her, and she almost called out to him. But she forced herself to stay silent, because she was pretty sure one more appeal wouldn't make any difference. He was hiding too much, and she'd made the right decision, she told herself as she watched him drive out of the parking lot and head toward town.

Chapter Six

Mark could feel Molly's gaze drilling into his back. He ached to turn around, climb back into her car and pull her into his arms. He pictured his hands stroking her back, pictured himself pressing her face against his shoulder as he told her who he was and that he wasn't going to let Bauder or Hammer get at her.

Even though he wanted to reassure her, there was too much at stake to give her any assurances. Like his whole future. Despite the temptation, he couldn't simply trust her with his secret. And beyond that was a nagging doubt that as soon as he told her who he was, she'd accuse him of outright lying to her, to which he'd have to plead guilty.

So he forced himself to drive out of the parking lot without looking back. Really, she was right to send him away. As far as he could tell, she was being honest with him, and he couldn't do the same with her. Not now. Maybe not ever. She might be the woman of his dreams, but in reality a relationship was going to be impossible.

Feeling like a vise was squeezing his insides, he went back to the very nicely appointed East Point

Lodge, where he poured himself a scotch on the rocks from the minibar in his room.

He took the drink out to his private balcony overlooking the ocean, lowered himself into a lounge chair and sat staring morosely at the breaking waves. The lodge was on the ocean side of the spit of land where Perry's Cove had been built. On the other side was the sound. And in some places the land between the two bodies of water was only a few blocks wide. It was a very fragile environment.

When he'd lived here, he'd been like all the other residents—playing Russian roulette with the forces of nature. Now he saw the picture somewhat differently. As he sat watching the waves roll up the beach, he was thinking it might be better if Perry's Cove simply washed out to sea.

One harrowing afternoon in town had convinced him he was never going to make his home here again. All he wanted was to find out who had killed Veronica and prove it. Then he'd find some other community more to his liking and go back into business. He'd already invested some of Veronica's insurance money, and it was bringing in a nice little income. So he wasn't going to have to work his buns off to make a living. He could start low-key with a few quality houses and let his new community find out what kind of product he built.

As he sipped his scotch, he pictured himself living in a small city somewhere in the South, since he'd gotten used to a warm climate.

And as the image built, he started thinking about a woman at his side. It was Molly Dumont, of course. The fantasy wife he'd conjured up for himself.

He started out with a nice simple image of the two

of them carrying in groceries, putting food away, talking about whether to have grilled salmon or barbecued ribs for dinner. But the scene didn't simply stay cozily domestic for long. He reached for her, she came willingly into his arms, and he slipped back into the kind of fantasy that had kept him from going crazy during the long nights in prison.

In his daydream he pulled up her knit top, unhooked her bra and took the weight of her breasts in his hands, stroking her, giving the two of them pleasure. Then he lowered his head and buried his face in her softness. For years he had only imagined those breasts. Now he had felt them pressed tightly against his chest, and he knew their size and shape.

In seconds he was aroused, his breath shaky and uneven, his body ready for sex. He might have slipped further into the fantasy, but the sound of a dog barking down on the beach brought his mind back to reality.

He sat up straighter and scrubbed his hands across his face. Lord, what was he doing? Molly Dumont was only a few miles from where he sat, lusting after her.

Had he lived so long in his fantasies that they had become a habit he couldn't break?

If anyone else had described this situation to him, he would have thought the guy was pathetic. All he had to do was get in the car and drive to Molly's house. Again he pictured the two of them embracing. She'd kissed him this afternoon with uncontrolled passion. He wasn't making up that response. But it wasn't as simple as two people who wanted to make love with each other. Before anything could happen, he'd have to level with her. And he wasn't prepared to do that.

He cooled down his overheated body with images of Dean Hammer and Bill Bauder squeezing him for information back at the Randall house. If he'd just walked into the situation, he'd think the two of them were working together—for some purpose he didn't yet understand.

Did they have some vision of an idealized Perry's Cove, where only the right people were going to live in their carefully controlled community? Had they made an executive decision that Mark Ramsey was the wrong sort?

Or was their purpose more sinister? He'd find out. But he'd do it carefully, because he knew that they were both dangerous and powerful in this small community.

He kept Molly Dumont out of his mind as he ate his evening meal in the lodge's excellent dining room. The rack of lamb, grilled romaine and perfectly roasted Yukon gold potatoes were excellent. He couldn't stop himself from topping off the meal with crème brûlée.

It had been an eventful day. After watching the evening news, he turned off the lights. He might be able to master his waking thoughts, but his dreams were beyond his control. This time his relationship with Molly wasn't the feature attraction. Instead, he was back in prison. Finally, in the middle of the night, he clawed his way back to consciousness and lay in the darkness, sweat pouring off his body.

The prison setting was vividly familiar. But this time his captivity had come with an all-new twist. Instead of Big Louie and the other sadistic guards, the players had been different.

Dean Hammer had taken Big Louie's role. Bill Bauder had been one of his helpers, along with Cory Daniels. He didn't have to be a psychiatrist to figure out what the dream meant.

There was something else, too. Molly had been in the dream. She'd been trying to get to him, begging the guards to leave him alone, and they'd shoved her back, put a solid barrier of flesh between himself and her.

He understood that part, too.

So was it true? *Would* she defend him?

He clenched his teeth and gathered up handfuls of the rumpled sheets, because what he wanted to do was pick up the phone and call her. But what the hell was he going to say? That he wanted to confirm his dream appraisal of her motives?

Instead, he heaved himself out of bed, stood for a long time under a warm shower, then tested the toe he'd banged up yesterday. It didn't hurt, so he dressed in shorts and a T-shirt and headed outside for a six-mile run along the beach, the wind blowing back his hair as his feet pounded the firm sand along the line of waves. He'd had this fantasy in prison, too. Freedom. The sun warm on his skin, the wind blowing in his hair, the tang of salt air in his nostrils. Then he'd wake up to the reality of a small dark prison cell filled with the odor of too many men crowded together into a too-small space.

He clenched his fists, blocking out that image as he speeded up his pace. By the time he made it back to the lodge, he was breathing hard and his skin was slick with sweat again. But it was good sweat, not the cold sweat of nightmares.

Showered again, shaved, and dressed in new chinos and a comfortable knit shirt, he asked the concierge about the condos he'd seen up the road—the condos he and Molly had visited yesterday. It turned out the guy's brother was working at the project for the summer, and the builder was Tilden Construction.

Tilden again. Very interesting.

The lodge complex included a group of shops and restaurants arranged along low boardwalks and wider deck areas. Mark bought an iced latte at the coffee shop, then sat at an umbrella table looking out over the landscaped grounds while he contemplated what he'd just learned.

Six years ago Tilden had been hot to develop property on the north side of town, and Veronica had headed the committee that petitioned the zoning board to block the project. They'd been successful, and Jerry Tilden had been pretty angry. Angry enough to kill?

It hadn't entered Mark's head at the time. With what he had seen recently, he was starting to wonder.

Suppose the developer had been furious with Veronica back then—and now he had Molly in the crosshairs?

The notion made him go cold. He didn't want to believe it was true, yet it looked as if Molly had been targeted twice for accidents—both times at Tilden projects.

He was in the car and driving to Tilden's office before he'd formulated a plan. Then in the reception room, he heard himself telling the secretary that he was doing research for a book on the area and wanted the perspective of one of the leading builders.

The story had the desired effect on the little redhead manning the desk in the front office.

After asking Mark to take a seat, she hurried down the hall. Five minutes later the man himself strode into the reception area.

He was about as Mark remembered him. Tall and broad-shouldered, going to fat in the middle, and with his brown hair pulled back in a ponytail to compensate for the thinness on top, a look Mark had always despised.

He held out his hand, and they shook.

"So you're writing a book about the area," he said without questioning the cover story or even asking Mark's name as he led the way to his private office.

Amazing, Mark thought as he smoothly elaborated on his nonexistent thesis. "Yes. I want to do a study of a small southern town where tourism is one of the main industries."

"Well, Perry's Cove fills that bill," the developer replied as they both took seats, Mark in a guest chair and the builder behind a large teak desk.

"Can you give me an idea of how development has speeded up in the past few years? If it's speeded up."

"It sure has." Tilden rattled off some figures, which Mark wrote down. The numbers were frightening. If development kept up at this pace, there would be no open land left between the sound and the ocean.

"So is getting good help a problem?"

Tilden's gaze sharpened. "Why do you ask?"

"I was in the downtown area yesterday, and I saw someone knock a bucket of shingles off a roof of a store being remodeled. It turned out to be one of your projects."

A worried look flickered across Tilden's face, but it was quickly masked. "Are you the guy who pushed Molly Dumont out of the way?"

"Yeah."

"Funny you didn't mention that when you came in.

If you're writing a book, I think you're trying to make me look bad. You and—'' He stopped abruptly.

''Me and who?''

''Forget it. What are you going to do, write about that roofing incident?''

''If it's relevant.''

Tilden stood up. Mark did the same.

''You can say that I'm known for my excellent construction. And if I see anything libelous in your book, I'll sue your ass off. If you want to highlight a guy who cuts corners, write about Randall, the owner of the murder house.''

''I did some research on him,'' Mark said mildly. ''That's why I wanted to see the house.''

''Well, did you run across the fact that he did a crappy job of renovating an old fish-processing plant into an antique mall?''

''No.''

''Research that.''

''I will,'' Mark answered tightly. He knew his workmanship on the damn project had been excellent. So why was Tilden doing a number on a guy who wasn't here to defend himself? Had something happened out at the antique mall or was Tilden trying to deflect Mark's interest in himself? He sure as hell was going to find out.

''Thanks for your time,'' he said as he started for the door.

''You'd be well advised to pick some other town for your little research project.''

Mark stopped and turned. ''Is that a threat?'' he asked, seeing Tilden's hands balled into fists at his sides.

''Of course not. Just some well-meaning advice.''

Mark's features were set as he marched through the front room. He could hear Tilden's footsteps behind him, and forced himself to keep walking, all the way to the car.

He was sitting behind the wheel, wondering what to do next, when a black-and-white cruiser pulled up next to him. He went rigid.

Cory Daniels, the deputy who had been with the sheriff the day before, climbed out and approached him.

He rolled down his window. "Can I help you?"

"Step out of the vehicle, please."

Mark complied, his heart rate suddenly skyrocketing. Images from last night's dream flashed into his mind, only now it was a waking nightmare.

"Spread your legs and place your hands on the top of the car," Daniels directed.

"Now wait a minute!"

"You have two seconds to comply," the deputy said.

Mark complied, feeling a crawling sensation like insect feet on his neck as he felt the man pat him down.

A century passed before Daniels murmured, "This is your lucky day. You're clean."

Mark forced himself to stand there without comment because he knew anything he said now could and would be used against him.

"You're best advised not to harass Mr. Tilden," Daniels said. "And best advised to get out of town."

That pronouncement did provoke a response. "I thought Sheriff Hammer wanted me to stick around."

"Oh, the house thing? We found a dead deer in the

bedroom. It crashed in through a picture window, cut itself up and bled to death."

Mark breathed out a small sigh. So he was off the hook on that. He was even more relieved when Daniels got back into his cruiser and drove away. Mark climbed back into his car, resisting the impulse to wipe the sweat off his forehead.

Looking up, he saw that one of the slats on the building's front window was lifted. Someone in there was watching. Probably Tilden. He must have a pipeline to Deputy Daniels.

With a quick, jerky movement, he pulled out of the parking lot and drove away, his breath still uneven. Daniels had made him feel like a convicted felon again, and he didn't like the sensation.

He wasn't paying much attention to where he was going until he realized he was heading toward the real estate office. His automatic reaction to stress had been to seek out Molly. What if he went in and told her everything? He slowed down, then blinked as she stepped outside wearing a nicely fitted pantsuit. He'd wanted to see her. Only it wasn't quite how he would have wished, since she was with a good-looking guy dressed in a sports jacket and slacks.

In the midst of an animated discussion, the couple took no notice of him as he drove by.

The man was probably just another client, he told himself. Not a lover or a killer hired to do the job that yesterday's accidents hadn't been able to accomplish. The latter idea was doubtless outrageous. Yet once it popped into his head, he couldn't dislodge it.

The air-conditioning hadn't been working long enough to kick in, and it was still stuffy inside the car. But a sudden icy chill swept over his skin. Slowing, he watched in the rearview mirror as Molly pulled onto the highway, heading in the same direction he was going.

He took the next side road, where he made a quick U-turn. When Molly's car passed, he waited several beats before pulling out and following her and the man, dropping back when she slowed. His eyes flicked to the rearview mirror to make sure Deputy Daniels wasn't following him.

Several minutes later, Molly pulled into the parking lot of a popular restaurant, Madeleine's. Well-dressed men and women were getting out of cars and heading for the front door, and he realized that they were gathering for a meeting of one of the local professional societies. That meant the guy with Molly was probably not planning to drive her to a secluded stretch of beach where he could make love to her or kill her.

He started to drive by, then he decided he'd like to know what the group was saying about Mark Ramsey. Were they talking about his run-in with the sheriff? His trip to the Treasure Hunt Pavilion?

He didn't consider that he was looking for excuses to stay in Molly's vicinity as he pulled into the parking lot and found a space. Most of the guys getting out of cars were wearing sports coats or short-sleeved dress shirts with nice slacks and no tie. He looked down at his own knit shirt and chinos, thinking that he didn't exactly fit in. But that might not matter. Picturing the interior of the restaurant, he remembered there was a big meeting room in the back, near the rest rooms.

From the rear seat, he picked up a baseball cap and jammed it onto his head. The hostess was busy, so he was able to bypass the front of the dining room and follow a group of people down the hall in the back, then walk past the meeting room, which was filling up with local businesspeople, some of whom he recognized. There were tables set for lunch, but nobody had sat down yet.

Molly was chatting with several people, her back toward the door. He heard Ted Collins, the owner of a crafts store, asking her about the roof incident. Her answer minimized the accident, and he wanted to tell her she was taking the right approach.

"So later you got into some trouble at the old Randall place," Collins pressed.

Mark stopped just past the door, straining his ears to hear her answer to that one.

"No big deal," she replied, then switched the topic by asking if Ted was looking forward to the luncheon speaker.

The phones weren't far away, and he picked up the receiver, keeping his hand on the hook while he pretended to dial a number.

Face hidden by his hat, he hunched his shoulders, making himself as inconspicuous as possible.

From where he stood, he heard Mike Randall's name mentioned a couple of times. But he really wasn't close enough to find out anything useful. When he saw Bill Bauder come in, he decided that he could make better use of his time. If Bauder was here, then he wasn't going to be at his office, which meant that a researcher wasn't going to encounter him if he went over there and asked to see back issues of the paper.

He turned and started for the exit, then felt a tingling sensation as he crossed the wide doorway of the meeting room. Turning his head, he saw that Molly had chosen that moment to look up. Her eyes were locked on him, and he stopped in his tracks. The room was full of men and women, but it felt as if the two of them were the only two human beings in the universe. She was the one who broke eye contact first, deliberately turning toward the tables where others were already choosing seats.

He watched her walk toward a place setting, watched the man who had come with her take the seat next to her and put his hand familiarly on her shoulder.

That hand made Mark's stomach clench. Then he firmly reminded himself that he had no claim on Molly Dumont.

The guy was speaking to her. "Are you all right?" he asked.

"Yes, fine."

Mark stood with his hands stiffly at his sides, wanting to cross the room and ask her to leave with him. But he knew the impulse was totally irrational. It would be the worst possible thing he could do because it would draw attention to both of them.

So he forced himself to walk toward the front of the restaurant and leave. He'd come here on impulse, and probably that hadn't been a very good idea. But at least he'd pinned down Bill Bauder's location.

So his next stop was the office of the *Voice of Perry's Cove,* the rag that dominated the local media. Well, it was actually the *only* local media. There was no radio or TV station here, so Bill Bauder had made the *Voice* the place to look for detailed coverage of local events. That was how he had set himself up as a power in the community. People's views of you were influenced by Bauder's view. And if you got on the wrong side of him, you were likely to suffer publicly.

Mark wasn't sure what he had done six years ago to earn such virulent coverage in the *Voice.* It might make sense if Bauder was working with whoever had set him up. But what would the editor's motive have been?

The newspaper office was not in the central business district but in another converted factory about a quarter mile from downtown. The wood-frame building looked out of place in the residential neighborhood that had grown up around, but it was convenient for Bauder. There was plenty of employee parking and plenty of room to unload papers that came from the printing company on Wednesdays and Saturdays.

As Mark recalled, for a small-town paper the *Voice* had a fairly large staff. Ad salesmen were in greatest supply. But there were also a couple of part-time reporters and feature writers, even a food editor. But Bauder kept a firm hand on all aspects of the operation and he personally wrote what he considered the important stories.

A desk in the lobby of the building controlled access to the interior.

Manning the station was a petite woman who seemed barely out of high school, and he wondered if she was full-time or just a summer intern.

"Is it possible to look at your archives?" he asked.

"Yes, of course," she answered, then stared at him. "You're...the guy Mr. Bauder met at the old Randall place."

"How do you know?"

"Mr. Bauder's already developed the pictures. He's doing a new story for the Wednesday edition."

"Oh, dandy," he muttered.

"Don't you like being famous?"

"I came here for peace and quiet." He sighed.

"Just let me duck into the back room and look at those old editions."

"Okay. But you have to sign in and wear a visitor badge."

Just great, Mark thought. So Bauder would know he'd been there. But he signed the sheet and took the pass because he didn't see any alternative.

"What years did you want to see?" she asked as she led him to the room at the back where bound volumes of old editions were kept.

"I don't know. I'm writing a book about Perry's Cove, and I just want to get a feel for the town."

"Okay. We have a computerized index in case you want to look up a specific topic."

"All the modern conveniences."

When she'd finally left him alone, he got out some of the volumes with stories about the Randall murder, steeling himself to view the old articles. But it wasn't as bad as he'd thought it would be. He could look at them with detachment, as though he were reading about some other poor jerk who'd been chewed up and spit out by the system.

Curious, he went back to the index and looked for the latest article on Mike Randall. To his surprise, Bauder had reported the fact that the conviction had been reversed—in a small article buried on page seventeen. At least he hadn't omitted the information entirely.

Next he put Phil Dumont's name into the index. He was shocked to realize he was reacting more strongly to what he was seeing than to the previous subject.

He saw that Molly and Phil Dumont had been given the same sensational treatment as Mike and Veronica Randall.

There were pictures of the couple attending a dance sponsored by the merchants' association. Then pictures of a dazed-looking Molly next to stories of her husband's suicide.

Apparently he'd taken his life at the antique gallery. Not good for business, Mark thought. He could see why Molly had been forced to find another source of income. Probably the other dealers had been furious about Phil's parting shot, so to speak.

Mark sat back and thought about that phrase. When he'd been in prison, the wife of one of his fellow inmates had committed suicide, and the man had been so distraught that he'd also tried to take his own life. In order to understand what had happened, Mark had read a lot about suicide. An individual who took his life often saw his situation as hopeless. Ending his own pain might be his primary motivation, but there was also an element of punishment for those left behind. "See what I was forced to do. Now you deal with it."

It sounded as if Phil Dumont had been sending that kind of message to his fellow antique dealers, otherwise he might have picked a more private place to end his life.

Had Phil blamed the dealers for the failure of his business? Mark didn't know, but the antique mall brought him back to one of his original purposes in coming here.

He looked up more listings on the place and found that, indeed, there had been a couple of accidents. A stair tread had broken, injuring a tourist. A window had blown in during a thunderstorm. And a plumbing pipe had burst, ruining merchandise in one area of the gallery.

None of them were big problems, nor could Mark lay the blame on his construction. Poor maintenance was just as likely, he told himself, while still struggling with his feeling of discomfort.

He spent another half hour randomly looking at recent editions of the paper to ascertain the present tone. Then he figured he should get out of there before he bumped into Bauder.

After handing in his visitor pass and signing out, he headed back to his room at the East Point Lodge, to change from slacks into more casual shorts.

The room had been cleaned in his absence. But as he reached to open the drawer where he'd put his shorts, his hand stilled.

Someone had been poking through his stuff.

Chapter Seven

Mark stared at the drawer front with narrowed eyes. He'd listened to guys in prison talk about how to tell if their rooms had been tossed. So he'd mixed a little glue with some water and used it to paste strands of his hair against several of the dark-wood drawers, where they met the side of the dresser. On the drawer that held his sports clothes the hair was gone. So were all of the others, he discovered after a quick check.

The maid might have brushed against the dresser and knocked off one or two of the hairs. But not all of them, surely. Whipping away from the drawers, he hurried to the closet to inspect the box in which he kept the Mike Randall mask.

The combination lock was still in place, which proved nothing. If someone had figured out how to open it, they could have snapped it back into place when they finished.

He set the carrying case in the middle of the bed, wishing he knew for sure whether anyone had seen his little reverse disguise. If they had, they were doubtless wondering why a guy named Mark Ramsey had shown up in Perry's Cove with a Mike Randall mask.

He thought about locking the box in a self-storage

unit. There hadn't been any of those in town when he'd lived here previously, but perhaps that had changed. On the other hand, he'd have to show identification when he rented the unit, which meant that anyone following his movements would know about it and could break in, just as they'd gotten into the room.

Out in the hall, he went in search of the maid's cart. It was around the corner, about ten doors from his room.

As he waited by the door, she spotted him and came out.

"Can I help you sir?"

"I'm in room 203," he said. "You didn't happen to see anyone go in there, did you?" he asked, keeping his gaze on her face.

"No, sir," she answered quickly.

He pulled out his wallet. "I can make it worth your while, if you have any information."

As she eyed the wallet, he thought she might come up with something. But she only gave a quick shake of her head. Either she was honest and hadn't seen anything, or someone had already paid her to keep her mouth shut.

After that, he was too restless to stay around the hotel. As he headed back into town, he told himself it was time to judge the tone of the rumors about Mike Randall. So he drove straight to the Sea Breeze Café.

It was the place where old-timers hung out and tourists were viewed with suspicion. But he had the advantage of knowing whom to approach. So he took a seat at the bar next to Ray Myers, owner of the dry-goods store, where you could get everything from rubber rafts to hemorrhoid preparations. Besides dealing in dry goods, Myers liked to keep up on town gossip. And he was welcoming to outsiders, since his business depended as much on them as on the locals.

Mark knew that if he could get Myers on friendly terms, the others were likely to go along, at least enough to talk to him.

When he asked what was good, Ray recommended the North Carolina barbecue, and Mark ordered some, with sides of coleslaw and baked beans and a bottle of Duck Wing Beer, the local brew.

"Are you that guy investigating the Randall murder?" the store owner asked.

Mark blinked. "Where did you get that idea?"

"That's what they're sayin'."

"Well, I'm writing a book about the town, and the old murder is part of the story."

"And you got caught by the sheriff at the Randall house," Ray said, confirming his hypothesis that the story was all over town.

"I guess I was at the wrong place at the wrong time."

The tired-looking waitress, Pam Peters, set his beer and a glass in front of him. After carefully pouring himself some of the brew, he asked, "So, do you know what the sheriff found out about the blood in the Randall house?"

Myers looked him up and down. "Yeah. I do. A deer crashed through one of the back windows and cut itself pretty bad. It couldn't get back out."

At least people knew that nobody else had been killed there. Before Mark could get too pleased about that, Myers fixed him with a steady look and delivered a stern warning. "Molly Dumont don't deserve any more grief."

"I wasn't planning to give her any. I hardly know her."

Myers wiped his mouth on a paper napkin. "You found out about her husband?"

"I was reading about it over at the newspaper office."

The barbecue arrived, and Myers watched him take a bite. "What do you think?"

"I thought it might be sweet," he said, pretending the reaction he'd heard from northerners tasting this local treat for the first time.

"Nope. Vinegary is more like it."

"Yeah, but it's good." Mark chewed and swallowed another mouthful. North Carolina barbecue was one of the things he'd missed powerfully in prison.

The regulars at the Sea Breeze Café drifted by to talk to Myers, many of them drawing Mark into the conversation. He knew they were curious about him, and he did his best to answer questions, using the background he had made up for himself. He was from up north—which was basically true. He moved around a lot. He had inherited money from his grandfather, so he could afford to indulge his writing habit.

Funny. He didn't have any problem giving all this false information to the gang in town. It was different from the way he'd felt about lying to Molly.

Pam had set the bill in front of Mark. He reached for it, read the total and pulled his wallet from his back pocket.

"It's been good talking to you," he said to the room at large, then turned to Ray. "And if you think of anything you want to tell me, here's my e-mail address." He handed over one of the Mark Ramsey business cards he'd had printed. "Or contact me at the

East Point Lodge,'' he added and gave his room number.

''Until Molly Dumont finds you a house to rent,'' Ray said.

He didn't correct the impression because that would lead to too many explanations. Or maybe he didn't want to say that she'd told him to find another real estate agent because he didn't want that decision to be final.

Of course, the remark started him thinking about Molly again. In truth, she was always somewhere in his mind. After finding out how his every move was being reported, he had to wonder if the apparent attacks on her had something to do with himself. Was he the intended target?

That made no sense, not the first time, anyway. He'd been several yards from her when the bucket had fallen off the roof. But the second time...

He supposed somebody could have come after him. But what would have been the reason? He'd just arrived in town, and as far as he knew, nobody had been aware of him as anything but a writer looking to settle down for a few months.

On the way to his car, he paused for a moment. The late-afternoon sun was still shining brightly, but he felt a shiver travel over his skin. Casually, he looked around, caught by the feeling that someone was watching him. But he could see no one. So he walked to his car and exited the parking lot, thinking that it might be a good idea for Mark Ramsey to make himself a little less conspicuous.

FROM INSIDE one of the nearby shops, two men watched Mark leave the café and head for his car.

"Who the hell is he?" the older one asked in a voice that was edged with anger. "We don't need him here, stirring up trouble."

"I've started an Internet search. There's not much information on him. He's got a Maryland driver's license and an address outside Baltimore. He's got a good credit rating."

"He says he's a writer."

"Well, I checked on Amazon. They have every book in print and a lot that are out of print. If he's written anything, it's under a different name."

"Can you check magazines? Other publications? Maybe this is his first book."

They both watched Ramsey get into his car and drive away. "Where did he grow up? Where did he go to school?"

"I couldn't find that."

"Do you think Ramsey's his real name?"

"I'd like to know."

"I kind of thought Mike Randall might have shown up in town," the older man said in a hard-edged voice. "I was looking forward to killing him."

"I think he sent this guy instead. Too bad for him."

"You have something specific in mind?"

"Yeah, I do, because I'm not going to sit still and have him screw up the good thing we've got going."

EVEN AFTER the way they'd parted, Molly half expected Mark Ramsey to call her. When he'd happened to show up at Madeleine's, they'd exchanged an endless look, but he'd said nothing. She didn't know whether she wanted to talk to him, but every time the phone rang, she jumped.

At home, there were a couple of calls that she wondered about. Calls where she was sure someone was on the other end of the line but they said nothing. She checked her caller ID. The first time there was no readout because the battery was low. The next time all she saw on the screen was the annoying designation Unavailable.

She told herself it wasn't Mark. He wasn't the type of guy who would call and then not speak. But she kept thinking that the calls might have given her an excuse for contacting him. He'd suggested that somebody could be after her, and she'd discounted that theory out of hand. But he didn't know that.

The ploy was tempting—too tempting. Which was why she warned herself not to do it.

She was thinking about him too much. The haunting feeling that they'd known each other at some time in the past wouldn't go away, although there was no rational reason for that beyond her own overactive imagination.

It was unproductive to get all wound up with him, she told herself firmly. Whatever he wanted or didn't want to tell her about his past, there was no future with him, because he wasn't planning to stay in Perry's Cove.

So she was annoyed at her reaction Monday morning when she walked down the aisle of the dry-goods store and saw him standing by a display of potato chips, cookies and other products that weren't on the USDA-recommended list.

As though he knew she was there, he turned, and she saw his features light up with the same pleased expression she was pretty sure was plastered across her face.

"You eat junk food?" she asked, because she didn't want to stand there just staring at him.

"When I'm writing."

"You're working on your book?"

"Yeah."

Could a conversation be any more inane? she wondered as she took a step forward.

"Watch it." He moved toward her and took her arm to stop her forward progress, gesturing to the display beside her. She looked down and saw a slender wooden rod that was sticking out from one of the shelves. It was sitting next to a box of pinwheels that was on the floor. Some kid must have taken one out, then shoved it in the shelf instead of putting it back where it belonged.

He kept his hand on her arm, and she could feel the impression of his fingers on her flesh as they stood staring at each other.

"I was going to call you," he said.

"Did you?" she asked.

"What do you mean?"

"Somebody called and didn't say anything."

His eyes narrowed. "It wasn't me."

Mrs. Monroe, the busybody wife of one of the fishermen in town, had rounded the corner and was looking at them with interest. Several people had already asked her about him, and she didn't want to generate any more talk.

"Let's get out of here," she murmured.

He followed the direction of her gaze, saw the woman looking at them and nodded. She watched him put back the bag of sour-cream potato chips that he was holding in his free hand.

"Aren't you going to buy them?"

"You saved me from the error of my ways."

She giggled as they made their way out of the store and across the parking lot. She didn't even know where they were going until they stopped beside his car.

"I missed you," he said.

"Did you?"

He reached out his hand toward her, then let it drop back to his side as though he was very well aware of the habits of small-town busybodies.

"What are we going to do?" she asked.

His eyes locked on hers, and she had the feeling he might have said, "Go back to my hotel room and jump into bed."

Instead, he murmured, "Look at real estate."

She was afraid she might have answered yes to the imagined suggestion if he had made it. So her voice was strained as she said, "Okay. Yes."

He cleared his throat. "You could leave your car here or you could take it back to the office."

"We'd better do that. Because if we're going to look at any properties, I need the key."

"Yeah, right."

The ride to the real estate office alone in her own car gave her time to clear some of the fog from her brain. All it had taken was one look at Mark Ramsey, and she'd been back where she started a few days ago.

She should tell him she'd changed her mind. But when they pulled into the parking lot, she said she was going to get the keys to several rentals.

"Don't write down where you're going," he said in a gritty voice.

"I won't," she answered, even as she struggled

with a tiny kernel of doubt. If he wanted to assault her, there would be no record of where they had gone.

But that wasn't the problem. The problem was that they both wanted the same thing.

She hurried inside and brought up the listings of suitable rentals. She'd overheard Doris Masters talking about a new place, the Thompson property. When she looked it up, the database said the house wasn't available yet. But the key was in the office. So she decided to have a look at it along with several others.

Mark was still in his vehicle when she came out, his hands wrapped around the wheel.

"Let me drive," he said.

"Why?"

"I'm one of those guys who hates to have someone else behind the wheel," he answered.

She suspected it might be more than that. She suspected he might be thinking that if someone was following them, he could get away more easily. And she knew he had forgotten the original reason for having her drive. She knew her way around here and he didn't. Or did he?

She gave him a tight nod, then climbed into the passenger side of the car.

You could tell a lot about a guy by his car. His was neat and clean. Like Mike Randall's car, she suddenly thought.

Her gaze shot to him.

"What?" he asked.

"Nothing."

"It's something."

"I was thinking your car is like Mike Randall's. I mean, clean, uncluttered."

He jerked to a stop in the act of backing out of the

parking space. "Are you fishing for information?" he asked.

"No."

"Good," he answered, turning the car around and heading toward the highway. "Which way?"

"Right. Go about three miles. You'll come to Frontage Road. Turn right again."

"Got it." He pulled onto the highway. "Did you find out what happened out at the Randall place?"

"Yes. A deer crashed into the house."

"I heard."

"Then why are you asking me?"

"I'm testing to see if your sources of information are as good as mine," he said, and she heard the teasing note in his voice.

"My agency is handling the cleanup. Where did you hear about it?"

"Deputy Daniels told me. After he patted me down."

She winced. "What did you do to get him on your case?"

"I asked Jerry Tilden a few questions about his work crews."

She stared at him. Before she could pursue the subject, he switched back to an earlier topic. "How's the cleanup going?"

"We've already had a maid service out there. And a glass-repair company."

"Good."

"Why do you care?"

"I hate to see property messed up." He kept his eyes on the road.

She watched him flick his gaze to the rearview mirror, then back.

"Are we being followed?" she asked.

"Not as far as I can tell. But maybe they have guys with cell phones stationed along the road."

She jerked her head toward him. "You're kidding, right?"

"Maybe."

They rode in tense silence until he made the turn onto Frontage Road. Then she directed him to a line of rural mailboxes. The house was up a long sandy driveway.

"Maybe I should have told you to let some air out of your tires," she said when his wheels spun in one particular patch of sand.

"Yeah."

"You've driven on sand before?" she asked.

"Yeah," he answered again but didn't volunteer any additional information.

The driveway branched off into two forks.

"Which way?"

"Left. If you go to the right you'll come to a couple of mansions on the beach. One has fifteen bedrooms. The other has twelve. They're rented out by the week. Like for fifteen thousand dollars a pop in the high season."

He whistled through his teeth.

The house she brought him to was considerably more modest. He kept going at a steady pace and made it over a sand dune sprinkled with clumps of sea oats and other scrubby vegetation.

Pulling up near the front door, he turned the car around before climbing out. Without looking at him, Molly marched to the door and fumbled with the key in the lock.

The door was in a covered, recessed entryway with

walls on two sides. She was aware of him standing right behind her, aware of his breath stirring her hair. When she couldn't get the key into the lock, he took it out of her hand and slipped it into her pocket.

"What are you doing?"

"This." He gently turned her to face him.

It registered that he'd made his move when they were still outside where they were less likely to get into trouble. But that was a relative term, she thought as she gazed into his smoldering eyes.

She had known from the moment she agreed to show him more property that something like this was going to happen. She had wanted it to happen. Even while she told herself she was being reckless, she raised her face to his.

There was a breathless moment when reality seemed to fade away, so that nothing remained in the universe besides the two of them—a man and a woman who had been fated to come together in this time and place.

When he'd first kissed her, it was as though she'd been seized by a whirlwind. This time he let her make the decision. She could turn around and walk back to the car if she wanted to play it safe.

Instead, she reached up to circle his neck with her arms. His lips came down on hers, slowly, as though he was making a monumental effort to keep his own needs within bounds.

His mouth brushed back and forth against hers, then settled gently, softly.

But that first touch was enough to shatter his restraint.

He went from gentle to hot and hungry in a heartbeat. She responded as she had the last time—with her own hunger leaping up to meet his.

He lifted his mouth a fraction, and she made a small sound of protest.

"I tried to stay away from you. It would be better if I stayed away from you," he whispered.

"Why?"

"Because I want you too much, and I don't want to hurt you."

She couldn't answer him. She knew he was right. He could hurt her badly. But there was no way she could pull back now.

She stood where she was, and when he gathered her closer, she forgot sanity and caution.

She had craved his distinctive flavor since their first kiss. Now she opened her mouth to savor him more completely. She tasted male hunger and dark, dangerous need.

His hands moved restlessly up and down her back, pressing her against the hard wall of his chest, so that she could feel the pounding of his heart. Or perhaps it was her own. She didn't know anymore. She only knew that she wanted to be with this man more than she had wanted anything in a long, long time.

She might have fled Perry's Cove after her life had been shattered three years ago. Now she was glad she'd stayed, because it meant she had met Mark Ramsey. She'd only known him a few days, yet, incredibly, it felt like a homecoming as his mouth sipped and nibbled at hers. It felt like a homecoming as his tongue played with the serrated line of her teeth before teasing more sensitive tissue beyond.

Her own tongue met his, stroking, teasing, inciting until they were both breathing in jagged gasps.

He angled her body away from his so that his hand could slip between them and cup one of her breasts.

She murmured her approval, then made a low sound of pleasure as he found her hardened nipple and took it between his thumb and finger.

"Oh!"

"I've dreamed of touching you like this."

"Yes." Since she'd met him, he'd been on her mind, starred in her fantasies.

He leaned back against the wall, splaying his legs to equalize their height and bringing her center against his. She felt the hard shaft of his erection and moved against it.

He sucked in a sharp breath before his mouth came down on hers again. She mentally started making frantic plans to find a place where the two of them could get horizontal.

The thought brought her up short. What was she thinking?

She wrenched her mouth away from his, trying to get control of her breathing, of her emotions.

"We can't do this," she gasped out, taking a step back so that her body was no longer pressed tightly to his.

That was the right thing to do, she knew. But it felt wrong.

He made a sound of protest. "Molly."

"No."

His features contorted painfully, but he stayed where he was. His gaze was dark as he said, his voice more raspy than usual. "You want me as much as I want you."

She sucked in a breath and let it out before answering. "I think that's pretty obvious. But despite what I might have led you to believe, I'm not the kind of woman who deliberately gets involved with a man when there's no future in the relationship. You're going to leave Perry's Cove, and I'll still be here."

"You don't have to stay. You could come with me."

"What?" She tried to wrap her mind around what he'd just said. "You're asking me to pick up and leave with you?"

He looked embarrassed, as though he hadn't meant to blurt out the suggestion. But he didn't try to take it back. "It's an option."

"I...can't."

"What's holding you here?"

She had no real answer to that question. Sometimes she hated this place. Sometimes she thought that she stayed here out of habit. Or fear of the unknown. But her ties to Perry's Cove weren't the only issue. "I can't go off with a man I hardly know."

He gave a tight nod, then started to speak in a low, halting voice. "Suppose I told you that I'd been here before. That I'd seen you and that I couldn't get you out of my mind."

She stared at him, openmouthed. "You're not making that up?"

"I'm not making it up," he said. The words did have the ring of truth.

"Where did you see me?"

"The antique gallery. You and your husband had the section on the middle left. I watched you for a long time."

"I don't remember you."

"You were busy."

She nodded, then said, "You thought I was married, yet you came back to see me."

"Not just for you. But you were part of it. I'm sorry

Phil...died. I know that was hard on you. But I'd be lying if I said I was sorry you're free."

She digested that, taking in all the implications, then asked, "I'm one of the reasons you came back. What are the others?"

The stone wall dropped back into place. "I still can't talk about that."

"Oh, right. Pardon me for asking." Because she didn't know what else to do, she whipped away from him and fished in her pocket for the key. Inserting it into the lock, she finally got it to turn and pushed the door open.

She had been in a lot of empty houses, and this one smelled wrong. As though someone had been here recently.

Cautiously, she stepped into the living room, then stopped short, her eyes widening in surprise.

Chapter Eight

Mark came in the door right behind her. The blinds were drawn, making the light low. Under the windows, out of view, the wall was lined with wooden crates about three feet long and two feet wide.

"This place is supposed to be empty," she said.

"Yeah. Those look like shipping crates. I'd say somebody's using this house for a storage depot." He stepped around her and headed for the boxes.

With a kind of desperate speed, she lashed out a hand and grabbed his arm, her fingers digging through his sleeve and into his flesh. "No!"

"I want to find out what's in there."

Her answer was quick and sharp. "And I want to get the heck out of here before Bill Bauder comes over the hill and starts questioning us again."

"You think that's going to happen?"

"With our luck, yes."

Her logic wasn't perfect, yet he could identify with the sentiment, since they were probably experiencing the same tingling feelings at the back of their necks. They'd been caught once. He didn't want another confrontation. And he certainly didn't want her involved again. Maybe the best compromise would be to clear out now, then come back on his own after dark.

"Okay. Give me a minute."

"For what?"

"At least let me look for shipping labels."

She nodded, but he could feel the tension radiating off of her as he walked to the nearest boxes, took a handkerchief from his pocket and covered his hand before turning the crate. As far as he could see, there was nothing to identify the sender or the receiver or the contents.

"Nothing," he muttered.

"Maybe this is where the church auxiliary stores the Christmas decorations."

"Yeah, right."

"Please, I want to leave."

"Okay."

"Thank you."

"For not being a bullheaded macho male?"

"Something like that."

"I'll do you one better," he answered, using the handkerchief to wipe the edge of the door where she'd touched it.

"Isn't that kind of extreme?"

"As long as we're being safe, why not go all the way? I don't want to leave any evidence that we were here." After she relocked the door, he wiped the door-knob and the outside edge as well.

They got back in the car, and Mark started down the lane. They had reached the highway and turned onto the blacktop, when a police cruiser came speeding in the other direction and took the turnoff at a rapid clip.

Both of them saw who was behind the wheel. Dean Hammer.

Mark swore under his breath. If Molly hadn't insisted that they leave the place, they'd be standing there flat-footed right now.

"You have excellent instincts," he said.

"I didn't know how excellent."

"This property was listed for rent?" he asked.

"Well..."

"Well, what?"

"It wasn't supposed to be available yet. But the key was in the office."

"Uh-huh."

"What's that supposed to mean?"

He countered with another question, watching her carefully. "What do you think is going on?" If she'd been involved in some shady business in Perry's Cove, she would never have taken him to that house. Would she?

She sighed and answered his spoken question. "I wish I knew."

He nodded, thinking that either the sheriff was involved or he was hot on the trail of the bad guys.

"Do you want to look at any more property?" she asked, her voice not quite steady.

"I think I've had enough excitement for today."

She nodded, and he headed back to the real estate office. But when she got out to start her car, the engine wouldn't turn over.

He climbed out of his own vehicle and walked to hers.

"Your car was fine when you left it?" he asked.

"As far as I know. I'm not great with internal combustion engines."

"Do you want me to have a look under the hood?"

"I'd be grateful." She reached down and popped the latch, and he opened the hood and propped it up.

Through the window, he saw someone watching them. But he couldn't tell who it was, and he lost interest in the office interior when a police car rolled into the parking lot. Dean Hammer was inside. Apparently he'd left the house with the boxes almost immediately, maybe because he'd found nobody there. He pulled up beside them and rolled down his window.

"You folks having some problems?" he asked.

"Yes," Mark answered as he and the sheriff eyed each other.

Hammer opened his door and slowly climbed out of the cruiser. As he ambled over toward Mark, he said, "Were you looking at more rental property?"

"Yes."

"You visit the Thompson house?"

"Yes," Mark answered before Molly could say anything. "Unfortunately, the key we had didn't fit the door."

Hammer stared at them as if he expected a confession that they'd been using the house to store illegal goods.

When neither of them accommodated him, the sheriff got back into his cruiser. Mark held his breath, silently wishing that the man would drive away. Instead, he pulled into a parking space, then went into the real estate office.

"What's he doing here?" Molly whispered.

"Hell if I know. But I'd like to leave before he comes back out."

"I'm with you. I can have a mechanic take a look at my car later."

Mark closed the hood of Molly's car. She got out and came over to his vehicle, then looked back toward the office.

"Would you give me a ride home?" she asked.

"Sure," he answered, keeping his voice neutral. He understood why she'd decided not to go inside. He hadn't liked meeting up with Hammer, either, although the encounter had been a bit more pleasant than his run-in with Daniels. Still, Molly's engine trouble and the sheriff had given him an opportunity he'd been wishing for. He'd wanted to see her home, but he hadn't thought it appropriate to invite himself over.

She directed him back toward Perry's Cove. He remembered that she and Phil had lived in one of the nicer sections of town, but apparently she'd moved to a cheaper area.

They pulled up in front of a small house that wasn't exactly falling apart, but he saw that the exterior needed a fresh coat of paint.

He pulled into the driveway and cut the engine, and they sat for a moment.

"I'd like to invite you in for lunch," she finally said.

"I'd like that."

"If we can avoid getting into another clinch."

"That's pretty direct."

"I think I have to be, after what happened a while ago."

"All right."

"You're agreeing to the ground rules?" she asked.

"Yeah. At least I know you trust me to come inside."

She gave him a tight nod and exited the car, and he knew he was treading on thin ice. She might trust him, but he didn't know if he could trust himself. Still, instead of saying he'd changed his mind, he followed her to the side door because he was hungry for information about her.

They stepped into a small kitchen that was outdated but spotless. It adjoined a dining room furnished with only an old oak table and four chairs and a Japanese sideboard.

He stood there, shocked in some basic way that he could hardly articulate. One thing he'd remembered was the cozy, comfortable home she'd created. Not only had she moved out of her old house, but she'd apparently been forced to strip her surroundings to the bone.

He gestured toward the sideboard. "That's nineteenth-century, right?"

"How do you know?"

"The quality of the lacquer. The inlay work."

"You know antiques?"

"Some," he allowed.

"How?"

"My parents were in the business."

"So, are you a collector?"

"When I was a kid, I collected old marbles and baseball cards."

Her face took on a wistful expression. "For me, it was Sandra Sue dolls. I liked them better than Barbie. Then I grew up and graduated to Queen Anne furniture."

"Yeah, I always liked that period. I—"

He had started to say that he and Veronica had had a Queen Anne bedroom, then thought better of it. He'd been enjoying the talk, actually. It was a far cry from what passed for jail-yard conversation.

Molly had turned toward him as though she was waiting for him to say something more about himself. He ached to fill in the blanks, or to refer to one of the talks they'd had long ago in his previous life as Mike Randall. He remembered them all—the words and the emotions.

At one of the antique dealers' parties, they'd discussed her ideas for remodeling her house. She'd wanted a bay window for plants, and he'd worked up an estimate for her. But then she'd told him Phil had put a hold on the project.

Another time, when he'd stopped by to see Veronica at the Treasure Hunt Pavillion, she'd been busy with a customer, and he and Molly had gone out to lunch. He'd felt like a teenager on a date.

Now the need to tell her that and everything else was like floodwater building up behind a dam. The impulse didn't simply come from guilt. It came from a conviction that he and this woman had traveled over important common ground—and all he needed to do was reach for her hand and continue the journey.

It was so tempting that his insides ached. But he told himself the impulse to open up to her was a trap. He couldn't allow himself that luxury. He had come to Perry's Cove with an important mission and he couldn't jeopardize it because Molly Dumont had suddenly become more important than revenge.

She stood there watching him, and he was glad that he'd learned to keep his expression calm even when his insides were churning.

The moment stretched, and when he didn't speak, she filled the silence. "Before Phil died, I had a lot of good pieces. I had to sell most of them to pay off our debts. I managed to hang on to a few favorites. Unfortunately, I've had to stick things where they don't really match."

"Don't apologize. You're coping better than most people could."

"Don't make me out as brave or noble. I've just done what I had to do to survive."

She walked into the kitchen, and he watched her open the refrigerator. Fate had dealt her a pretty raw hand, and she was playing it the best she could. He had no right to come into her life making demands. He should back right out the door, he thought, but he stayed rooted to the spot.

"Do you like Greek salad?" she asked.

"Yes."

She searched around the refrigerator and the cupboards. "I like to add protein, but it looks like the only thing I have is canned salmon. Does that work for you?"

"Sure," he answered. He'd never had Greek salad with salmon, but he was willing to try it. Hell, he was willing to try anything if it kept him close to her. Even if he'd promised not to start anything. "What can I help you do?" he asked, because he thought he'd be better off keeping busy.

"You cook?"

"When I have to."

She handed him a red onion and a knife. "Slice this."

His hands worked, but he was aware of her every

movement as she quickly put together the simple meal. After a while, he realized she'd spoken to him.

"Would you like iced tea with lunch?"

"Fine."

She brought the pitcher of tea from the refrigerator while he carried the cutlery to the table.

She was coming into the dining room with two bowls of salad as he turned back to the kitchen, and they brushed against each other. Both of them drew in a quick breath.

"Sorry," they both said.

"You're sure you want me here?" he asked.

"Sit down and eat your lunch."

He sat and forked up some salad. It was good, better than he had expected.

For several minutes, they each concentrated on the food. The sound of his stirring sugar into his iced tea seemed to reverberate through the room.

It flashed through his mind to admit that he'd come to Perry's Cove to investigate the Mike Randall case. But then what? She'd want more information, and all he could give her was half truths or outright lies.

He sighed. "I know you want to know all about me. But I can't tell you. I also know that makes it difficult for the two of us to have a relationship."

"Not difficult. Impossible."

He had vowed not to press her, but he found himself saying, "When I hold you in my arms, doesn't it feel right?"

"It feels like I'm betraying myself. I can't have a relationship in a vacuum."

"Some people can. They meet on a cruise ship and make love because that's what they both want to do."

He watched her tongue flick over her bottom lip.

"We're not on a cruise ship, we're in the town where I live."

Her tone and the expression on her face made him want to tell her things he shouldn't. Instead, he stood and walked into the living room. Like the dining room, it was sparsely furnished. The sofa and easy chair looked like garage-sale purchases that replaced the comfortable pieces he remembered. But the coffee table was a beautifully restored sea chest, and a Victorian whatnot sat in the corner. Several pieces of china and cut glass decorated the shelves—along with something else that caught and held his attention.

It was a Chinese puzzle box about six inches long and eight inches wide, the kind where pressing on certain panels gets them to slide open. As he looked at it, he felt the hairs on the back of his neck stir.

Keeping his gait slow and steady, he walked to it, picked it up. He had seen it before—in his own house. Long ago Veronica had found the piece at a flea market and gotten it for a ridiculously low price. Maybe the box was broken, because neither of them had ever been able to work the mechanism.

Was he mistaken? Was it just a similar box? He turned the antique in his hand. It was polished wood, inlaid with ivory, and at the back was a small place where one of the ivory pieces had fallen out. The same place where Veronica's box had been damaged.

He pivoted back toward Molly. "Where did you get this?"

"It was Phil's. He gave it to me."

"It's a very unusual piece. Do you know where it came from?"

"From a dealer going out of business, Phil said." She was watching him, her head tipped slightly to one side. "Why do you want to know?"

Because he couldn't tell her the truth, he said, "A long time ago my parents had one like it. It always fascinated me. I kept trying to open it, but I never could."

"Yes. Sometimes I pick it up and play with it, but I can't figure out the combination."

He tried to remember the last time he'd seen the box, even while he wanted to bombard her with more questions. The box had been one of Veronica's treasures, something she wouldn't have parted with willingly. Certainly not for money. She wouldn't have sold it to Phil, yet Molly was claiming that it had belonged to her husband. So had Veronica given it to him? Because they were on very close terms, intimate terms? Had Phil taken advantage of the chaos after her death and stolen it? Or was Molly the one who had really acquired the box?

Suddenly he knew that he had come very close to making a serious mistake this afternoon. He'd almost let his attraction to Molly Dumont cloud his judgment.

Now he was back on track. He couldn't tell her who he was because it would be foolish to trust her.

"I'd better go," he said.

"Just like that?"

"You're the one who said it would be difficult for us to have a relationship."

"Yes."

"Then maybe it's better to walk away now." Before she could answer him, he did just that—walked out of the room and out of the house, where he got into his car and drove away.

FOR LONG MOMENTS Molly sat unmoving at the dining-room table. Something had happened. Something she didn't understand. One minute she'd thought Mark was on the verge of trusting her, the next, the gates of his fortress had slammed shut again.

She folded her arms across her middle, unconsciously hugging herself. When she realized what she was doing, she stood and picked up the two bowls that were still half-full of salad. She carried them to the kitchen and emptied them into the trash.

She'd been stupid, she told herself. She'd invited Mark in because she'd thought something might change. But it hadn't. That was pretty obvious. He was still closed up. And now he was also angry.

There had been an edge of anger in his voice when he'd asked her about the puzzle box.

Why? Had it triggered a painful memory? She didn't know and she suspected she was unlikely to find out.

She crossed to the living room and picked up the antique box. She was immediately conscious that Mark had cradled it in his hands only a few minutes ago, so that holding it now was somehow an intimate gesture.

Was she that starved for intimacy? a voice inside her asked.

Well, if she was, she could always pretend she and Mark Ramsey were amorous strangers who had met on a cruise. He'd made it clear that he'd go to bed with her anytime she said the word.

He *had* made that clear. Now she wasn't so sure, not after the way his expression had darkened so quickly.

Still cupping the box in her hands, she sat down on the sofa and turned it in all directions, thinking about when Phil had first brought it home.

He'd seemed pleased to have the piece, but he was always pleased when he got something for under the market price or sold something for more than it was worth. She'd understood the first because she shared his enthusiasm for a hidden treasure. But she'd never been comfortable jacking up prices of items beyond their value.

She shook the box, detecting nothing inside. But that didn't mean it was empty.

Again she tried to figure out the combination of moving parts that would open the secret compartment. But the sequence wasn't obvious, and she wondered if someone had glued the panels shut.

That would certainly devalue the antique.

So, had Mark seen this particular box before, perhaps, when he'd been at the antique gallery? Did he think there was something valuable inside? If so, what was he going to do, come sneaking back to the house to look? And was that why he'd been going around with her—because he was looking for something?

She didn't want to think that was true. And it couldn't be the only reason. He wanted her physically, she thought as the memory of their last heated encounter came sweeping back over her like a firestorm.

She gripped the box more tightly, trying to push that memory out of her mind. She had told him there wouldn't be any more intimate encounters between them. Intellectually, she meant it.

Now the problem was getting her body to go along with the edict.

IT WAS DARK when Mark drove past Molly's house again. He had made the decision to stay away from her, no matter how much he wanted to be with her. He reminded himself that he couldn't trust her. He reminded himself that she wasn't going to let him touch her again unless he told her why he was in Perry's Cove.

So why was he here, looking through the lighted windows, watching her in the kitchen fixing dinner?

Seeing her inside and knowing he couldn't cross the barrier between them made his hands clench on the steering wheel. With a low curse, he pressed on the accelerator and sped away, heading for the north side of town where they'd inspected the rental property that morning. This time he was equipped with a set of lock picks and some tools for breaking into the boxes.

When he reached the driveway, he switched off his headlights, then sat for several minutes, letting his eyes adjust to the dark, as he considered what he was about to do. He was taking a chance coming back. But it was an acceptable risk, he told himself, unwilling to examine his own logic too closely as he started the engine again and plowed forward.

Tonight he'd let some of the air out of his tires to make it easier to drive on the sand. Nevertheless, it was a nerve-racking ride up the driveway. In the distance he could hear loud music and party sounds. Apparently at least one of the mansions was rented, and the present occupants were making the most of their week at the beach. He took the fork to the mansions and parked with a bunch of other cars.

On foot, he circled back and approached the smaller house and waited for several minutes to make sure nobody was around, particularly Dean Hammer. Then he crossed the parking area and pulled on a pair of surgical gloves. The moon slid behind a cloud, and he switched on his flashlight so he could study the lock.

Nothing too complicated, he decided as he got out his picks. It took only minutes to open the front door.

The moment he stepped into the living room, he knew that he'd gone to a lot of effort for nothing. The boxes were gone.

He cursed under his breath, then walked to the wall where they'd been stacked. Stooping down, he swept his hand across the floor, but found nothing to indicate that the boxes had even been there.

Quickly he took a tour of the rest of the house. Three bedrooms, two bathrooms, a kitchen were all as empty as the living room.

He closed a kitchen cabinet, then crossed to the front door and stepped outside. He had barely closed the door behind himself, when a noise to his right told him he wasn't alone.

Chapter Nine

Instinctively going into self-protective mode, Mark ducked low, feeling a rush of air above his head as someone barreled toward him. The assailant had struck at him, but he avoided the blow by making himself a smaller target.

In the darkness, the man swore. He'd like to see the guy's face, Mark thought as he whirled, his hand lashing out and connecting with muscle and bone. All he could see was a bulky, featureless body. He was pretty sure the attacker was a large man and not too fast. When Mark landed another blow, the assailant went into a kind of desperate overdrive of flying fists and panting breaths. The furious effort managed to drive Mark backward as he sought to avoid the blows. A few landed, and he got in several of his own. Mark was about to surge forward again when he stumbled over a rock half buried in the sand and landed on his ass, the wind temporarily knocked out of him. By the time he managed to push himself up, he heard the sound of a car engine starting. Apparently the vehicle had been parked out of sight around the side of the house, which meant the assailant had been here the whole time.

Mark dashed toward the sound of the engine and was rewarded by a cloud of grit kicked up by the wheels as the vehicle crossed the parking space in front of the house and sped down the driveway at a dangerous speed. Grains of sand hit him in the face and mouth. Cursing, he wiped at his lips. The debris in his eyes was more of a problem. He knew he couldn't rub them. He opened his eyes to mere slits, ignoring the pain as he jogged to where he'd left his car. Working by feel, he fumbled for the bottle of water on the passenger seat. With his head tipped back, he poured the water onto his face, rinsing the sand and blinking to clear his vision.

By the time he had finished with the first-aid treatment, the other car was long gone. With a low curse he started his vehicle, then sped down the access road, knowing he was already too late—unless the bastard who had attacked him had somehow plowed into a sand dune.

No such luck. There were no cars on the driveway, and when he reached the highway, it too was empty.

He stared at the stretch of vacant blacktop, trying to get inside the assailant's head. Did he have friends in town he'd go to, or would he tear off in the opposite direction?

One theory was as good as the other, Mark decided as he turned left toward town.

A few miles down the road he saw another car and sped up. The driver was a woman—and he knew no lady had been tangled up with him. So he passed her and kept heading toward town. On the outskirts, he encountered several more cars. In one, a couple was making out—and making themselves a late-night hazard on the highway.

By the time he got into the nighttime traffic in the business district, he silently acknowledged that he was too late to catch up with whoever had been staking out the empty house.

On the way into town, he'd been trying to figure out who had jumped him. Had the guy been guarding the stash? That didn't quite make sense, because the boxes had already been cleared out. Maybe the guy had helped transfer the stuff and then been about to leave when company had come snooping around.

Stopped by a red light, he clenched his hands on the wheel, angry that he had missed a chance to get some information. But as he passed the combination service station–convenience store that had once marked the southern edge of town, he realized that he wasn't too far from the antique mall. With a renewed sense of purpose, he sped up. A few minutes later, he pulled into the parking-lot entrance farthest from the front door and let the car glide slowly by with the lights off. The side of the building that faced the street was dark, but when he cruised around the right side, he could see dim illumination shining through one of the windows.

He nosed the car to the edge of the lot, got out and walked quietly back toward the building, hoping he wasn't giving Dean Hammer or Cory Daniels another crack at him. He should go back to the lodge, he told himself. But he was too pumped up to obey the advice. He had come out tonight to get information, and he wasn't going home empty-handed if he could help it.

He exited the car, then crossed the parking lot and carefully stepped into the narrow stretch of crushed shells that had been spread under the window.

Lifting his head, he looked through the window.

The action he saw inside froze the soles of his shoes to the bed of shells where he stood. When he could move again, he ducked to the side of the window, although the precaution was pure reflex, since he doubted the occupants of the room were paying attention to anything besides each other. Cautiously, he took a second look and saw Oliver Garrison and a woman in a clinch. He couldn't see her face, only her back. She was wearing a dark-colored knit dress that molded her figure almost as tightly as the hand that Garrison had clamped around her ass.

This was Mark's first experience as a voyeur, and good manners dictated that he should turn away, but he couldn't help gaping at the antique dealer and his female companion. Oliver moved his mouth to her ear, saying something that made her laugh, although the sound didn't carry through the window glass. But Mark didn't need to hear her response. It was perfectly apparent that Oliver was suggesting taking the intimacy to a new level.

As Oliver unbuttoned the front of his companion's dress and buried his face between her breasts, she clasped the back of his head, holding him to her as he turned first to one side then the other to give her breasts equal attention.

Mark tried to identify the woman. Her shoulders were broad for a female, and she wore her blond hair short and curly. He could tell it was dyed, because the strands had separated in back, and he could see brown roots emerging near her scalp. Her neck was short, and her bottom was generous. There was something familiar about her, although he couldn't figure out what. She had a rather full figure, and he thought that losing twenty pounds probably wouldn't do her any harm.

He stopped analyzing her body type when Oliver bent her backward across the desk, leaning over her, then reached to undo the fly of his slacks. Before he could complete the action, the phone rang.

The woman raised her head as she looked at the phone. She said something that Mark couldn't catch. Oliver shook his head. It was obvious from their body language that they were arguing over whether to answer the phone or continue their present activity. From where he was standing, Mark couldn't tell which of them had taken which side of the argument.

Finally Oliver snatched up the receiver. Mark watched him listen, then respond, then listen again. Apparently, he didn't like what he was hearing. The woman was looking at him, and he spoke to her.

Mark cursed the glass between him and the interior scene. Both occupants of the room were obviously agitated by the call. They were talking at once now as the woman straightened her clothing, then turned to a large gilt-framed mirror on the wall and ran her fingers through her hair, fluffing up the curls, giving him his first look at her face.

He had expected that she'd be one of the antique dealers. But she wasn't, not unless she had joined the group after his time. Yet her features left the impression that he'd met her before. She was still saying something over her shoulder to Oliver as she hurried from the room.

Seconds later Mark heard a door slam at the back of the building. There was no good place to hide, but he pressed into the shadows against the wall as the woman emerged. She took a deep breath, crossed the parking lot, then climbed into a car parked under the trees. Luckily it was at the other side of the lot from him. She wrenched the car into reverse and backed up with a jerk. Within moments she was speeding toward the highway.

Mark debated following her, but he was more interested in Oliver, and he might have a good opportunity to get something out of the man now. He'd transferred the case with the mask to the trunk of his car. Suppose, now that Oliver was alone and upset, he met up with Mike Randall? That would definitely create some additional tension. Maybe it would make him blurt out some important information.

Mark had never used the mask before, although he'd practiced putting it on several times. But he'd better not do it in the dark, he told himself. So he drove to an all-night gas station. There was only one car beside the pumps when he pulled up next to the men's room and went in. After locking the door, he set the case on the sink and opened it. Goose bumps rose on his arms as he gazed down at the face lying on a bed of dark foam rubber, its eye sockets as empty and dead as a skull. He hesitated for a moment, then picked it up and shook out the wrinkles, feeling the rubber slap at his skin like cobwebs blowing in the wind.

He paused for a steadying breath, then opened the jar of special adhesive and began to dab it onto various parts of his face the way he'd been taught. He pressed the mask into place and smoothed the artificial skin against his features, working his way carefully to his hairline and below the curve of his chin.

The layer of rubber felt confining against his skin, as though it were a barrier between himself and the world, and he knew he couldn't wear the damn thing for very long.

For several heartbeats he kept his gaze downward. When he finally lifted his eyes to the mirror, he saw the face of Mike Randall. While the mask had looked spooky in its carrying case, it was nothing compared to how it made him feel now. He gripped the edge of the sink, fighting a feeling of disorientation. His throat constricted as he stared at his reflection, seeing Mike Randall, victim.

He wasn't that man! He wouldn't be that man. He had taken charge of his life. Suddenly, he wanted to explain that to Molly. Make her understand why he'd hidden the truth of his identity.

Then he reminded himself he'd stamped out of her house because he didn't know how she'd acquired the damn puzzle box.

But that was the least of his worries now. He was after big game—Oliver Garrison. It was Garrison's reaction he wanted.

Too bad he hadn't arranged to fake his own death, Mark thought as he put the top back on the jar of adhesive and packed up his equipment. If he'd died, then Randall's reappearance in Perry's Cove would be all the more spectacular. But he had the feeling that the effect would be good enough as it was.

He leaned closer to the mirror, smoothing out a few spots where the mask was wrinkled. Then he turned and unlocked the door and looked out into the parking lot. The other car was still at the pump, so he ducked his head and walked with crisp steps back to his car, stowed the suitcase and started the engine.

The brisk walk cost him. The fight earlier in the evening was making him stiff. Probably he should be back in his room with a couple of ice packs.

But he wasn't focused on his bruised body. A feeling of excitement clawed at the inside of his chest as he drove to the antique mall and pulled up across from the back door. The woman's car had not returned, he noted.

Climbing out of his vehicle, he strode to the window where he'd watched the couple. The light was still on, and he could see Garrison pacing back and forth, his gaze fixed on the phone. Apparently, he was waiting for news from his girlfriend. They were up to something, and it looked as if there had been a hitch in their plans. For example, what if they'd been storing a bunch of boxes in an empty house, and someone had come to investigate their cache?

Was that what had happened? Did the caller know it was Mark Ramsey? He couldn't discount that theory, Mark decided as he watched the antique dealer's jittery behavior.

Garrison was acting like a man in trouble, and Mark was determined to make sure more was on the way. With a feeling of satisfaction, he pulled on another pair of rubber gloves, and hurried to the back door. It was locked, but he remembered the mechanism wasn't state-of-the-art. Apparently, that hadn't changed. The lock picks were still in his pocket, and he used them with more dexterity than he'd employed earlier in the evening. The old burglars in the pen would be proud of him, he thought as he stepped into the building and quietly closed the door behind him. After waiting for his eyes to adjust to the darkness, he took a few more steps into the loading-dock area. Large pieces of furniture loomed around him in the dim light, and he stationed himself behind a large German hutch called a shrank, if he remembered correctly.

When he heard and saw nothing, he stepped around

the shrank and through a door into the back area of the gallery proper. His pulse was pounding now, and he felt a tiny trickle of doubt work its way into his mind. Maybe this wasn't such a good idea. What if Garrison called the cops?

Mike Randall would have time to get away, he assured himself, unless someone from the sheriff's department was cruising around the area. Looking for kids having sex in the parking lot? That was what Garrison had told him Hammer had come to talk about. But Mark was thinking now it was a lie.

Before he changed his mind, he took a couple of steps through the doorway into the storage area at the back of the gallery. He had been here with Veronica many times, and he knew the general layout of the large room.

First he found a small, decorative metal box and set it on the table beside him. Then he quietly unscrewed the two overhead lightbulbs so that they couldn't come on. Next he found a lamp that was sitting on a low chest. After screwing in one of the bulbs from the overhead fixture, he set the light on the table beside the metal box. Then he plugged the cord into a floor receptacle and gave the lamp a quick test. It worked.

A glance over his shoulder toward the loading dock assured him that he had a clear escape route. Satisfied with his preparations, he looked around for something that would make a fairly loud noise, then deliberately kicked his foot against a set of old fireplace implements. They gave out a dramatic rattling sound as the poker clanked against the shovel, and he ducked around the side of a large chest on chest, waiting with his heart in his throat for Oliver to come and investigate.

He didn't have long to stand there in the shadows.

''Is that you?'' Garrison called out. ''I didn't think you were coming back so soon.''

A sardonic smile flickered over Mark's lips. ''It depends on who and when you mean,'' he answered, keeping his tone conversational and making an effort to speak like the old Mike Randall. He could do it for short periods of time, but anything longer would be a strain on his vocal cords.

''Who's there? Show yourself,'' Oliver demanded, but his voice had taken on a quavery quality that spoiled any attempt at forcefulness. He was in the doorway now, and he reached to flip on the light switch. The action had no effect, and he cursed.

''Nothing to worry about. It's just an old friend come for a visit,'' Mark answered, then took a step forward and switched on the lamp beside him so that he was standing in a small pool of illumination.

''No!'' Garrison breathed. ''What do you want?''

''Information.''

There was a moment's hesitation before the antique dealer said, ''I don't have to tell you a damn thing.''

''You sound like you have something to hide.''

''You shouldn't have come back here.''

''You knew I would, didn't you?''

''I hoped you'd be smart enough to stay away.'' As Garrison spoke, he lifted the hand that had been pressed against his side, and Mark saw he was holding a very nasty-looking handgun.

Chapter Ten

His eyes riveted to the gun, Mark had time to mutter, "Aw hell," as he ducked behind the chest on chest. He'd always thought of Garrison as a wimp. Apparently the man had stiffened his backbone in the years since Veronica Randall's husband had left Perry's Cove in handcuffs.

Still, Garrison's reflexes weren't all that great. He fired seconds too late, splintering the wooden chest several inches from Mark's head.

Mark forced a laugh. "You're destroying a priceless antique," he shouted.

"What the hell are you doing here?" Garrison shouted back.

"What do you think, you old goat? I'm trying to find out who set me up. Was it you?"

"Don't be ridiculous," Garrison said, but the quaver in his voice did nothing to make his protest sound legitimate. "I'm going to call the police," he added.

"You do that. What are you going to get me on? You're the one with the gun."

"I'm shooting at an intruder."

"Which doesn't give you a license to murder, if I remember my jailhouse law studies correctly."

As he finished speaking, he tossed a metal vase across the floor. While Garrison was shooting at it, he ducked out the back door, profoundly glad that he'd parked close to the building this time. He was into his car and out of the parking lot in a flash. Looking back, he was glad to see that Garrison hadn't come out of the building.

As he drove with his right hand on the wheel, he reached up with his left and worked at the mask, loosening the glue so he could pull the rubber away from his face. He resisted the impulse to rip the damn thing off. It was too expensive to ruin after one wearing, although he was wondering how he was going to use it again, considering the outcome of this little episode.

When he realized his foot was pressed to the accelerator, he eased up. All he needed was to be caught speeding with his Halloween mask half off or on the seat beside him.

Now that he was out of the building, it was pretty clear that he never should have tried the mask stunt. He'd come to Perry's Cove with a disguise and a half-baked plan, only to find that he was no covert investigator. Probably he'd read too many Spenser for Hire novels, where Spenser went around a town stirring up trouble until people attacked him and he beat the crap out of them. It worked in the novels, but Mark wasn't so sure of its merits in real life.

He sighed as he headed back to the East Point Lodge, wondering if he'd magically come up with any insights overnight. On the way, he detoured past Molly's house again. The lights were off, and it was all he could do to keep from knocking on the door, waking her up and throwing himself on her mercy. He'd come to town with the burning desire to avenge himself on the bastard or bastards who had killed his wife and pinned the murder on him. As he drove through the night, he wondered if that was a goal worth pursuing. Maybe it was better to go on with his life and grab what happiness he could. With Molly Dumont.

A tide of longing seized him. At that moment he wanted her more than he'd wanted anything in his life. But he gritted his teeth and pushed the desire out of his mind. He had come back to Perry's Cove with a purpose and he wasn't going to quit in a moment of personal weakness.

Besides, tonight wasn't a total loss. In the process of almost getting himself killed, he'd learned something important. Oliver Garrison was afraid of Mike Randall, afraid enough to pull out a gun and shoot at him. He might have brought the gun out because he thought that a burglar had broken into the gallery. But he'd seen Mike, spoken to him. He knew who he was and still he had tried to kill him. That was pretty significant. And Mark couldn't simply walk away.

OLIVER'S HANDS were shaking as he returned to his office and slipped the gun back into the desk drawer where he kept it. From another drawer, he took out a bottle of brandy. Usually, he enjoyed the little ritual of pouring an inch of the golden liquid into an antique brandy snifter.

Tonight he tipped the bottle up and took a swig, welcoming the burning sensation in his throat. He leaned back in the comfortable desk chair, feeling the beating of his heart as he let the alcohol work its way into his system.

He knew that he was stalling, but he didn't give a

damn. Since the murder conviction had been overturned, he'd been waiting for Mike Randall to show up, and now it had happened. Not the way he'd expected. Somehow he'd pictured the man strolling into the gallery during the day as if he owned the place. But, after all, it had been Randall's privilege to choose his time and place.

Oliver sighed. He didn't know what Randall knew or what he suspected. Probably it was impossible for the sucker to figure out the truth on his own. He'd need help, and Oliver was going to make sure he didn't get it.

He took another swig of brandy. This time it was possible to appreciate the expensive flavor. He had always liked fine things. Good food and drink. Beautiful furniture. Expensive knickknacks.

It would be a shame if he were forced to give them up if he had to get out of Perry's Cove in a hurry. All that went through his mind as he sat sipping brandy. The drink calmed him, and he began thinking about how to put the brief encounter in the best possible light. He hadn't exactly kept his cool. Shooting at the guy hadn't been the best idea in the world, but he'd been betting that Randall wouldn't get a chance to tell his side of the story.

When he finally felt in control of his emotions, he reached for the phone and dialed a familiar number.

"Hello, it's me," he said after he heard the receiver picked up on the other end of the line.

"Oliver?" a voice asked. Then, in response to his tone of voice, "What's wrong?"

"I just had a run-in with Mike Randall," he said, knowing he was delivering a bombshell.

"When? What happened?"

"He showed up at the gallery a few minutes ago."

"You mean after midnight?"

"Yes."

"And?"

"I believe he was trying to create a dramatic effect. He unscrewed a couple of lightbulbs and arranged to have himself standing in a circle of light from a lamp."

There was silence on the other end. When the voice finally spoke again, it was angry. "So first he sent that guy Mark Ramsey. Now he's here, too, running around town, looking for trouble."

"That's right. And with your connections, you have an excellent opportunity to locate him."

Oliver endured several moments of invective, then calmly said, "If you can't find him, perhaps you can take a different approach."

"Like what?"

"Like cut off his sources of help. Mark Ramsey is going around with Molly Dumont. They were at the Thompson place earlier today. And Ramsey came back tonight to snoop around."

The man on the other end of the line cursed. "Why wasn't I informed of that?"

"I'm telling you now."

"You think Dumont knows something about our plans?"

"How could she?" Oliver snapped. But he was starting to wonder. Somehow, Molly was in the middle of this.

"Get her to tell you what's going on. Or if you don't want to do it yourself, use those guys I have on retainer. I'm tired, and I'm going to sleep," he lied.

He slammed the receiver into the cradle. No one was going to sleep tonight.

MARK CIRCLED around town, making sure he wasn't being followed before going back to the East Point Lodge. He was heading toward the door to his unit when the cell phone in his pocket rang, making him miss a step.

He stopped in his tracks, willing himself to steadiness. Who the hell could it possibly be? Had Oliver figured out who he was and gotten his number?

Impossible, he told himself. There was no way the antique dealer could figure out that Mark Ramsey and Mike Randall were one and the same. Still, when the phone rang again, goose bumps popped up along his arms.

It had to be a wrong number, he told himself. Even as the thought formed, he canceled it. The Light Street Foundation knew how to reach him. But why would they be calling him in the middle of the night? That left only one possibility, he thought as the phone jarred his nerves again. Pulling it out of his pocket, he pressed the Talk button.

"Hello?"

"Mark, thank God!"

"Molly, what is it? What's wrong?"

"I heard a noise outside. There's someone prowling around the house."

"Are the doors and windows locked?" he asked, already sprinting back toward the car.

"The doors and the downstairs windows."

"I'm minutes from your house," he said, keeping his voice calm as he climbed into the car and started the engine. "Where are you?"

"In the bedroom."

"Lock the door. And lock the window."

"Okay."

He heard her suck in a strangled breath. Then she screamed.

"Molly," he called into the phone. "Molly!" But she didn't answer. A wave of pure primal panic grabbed him by the throat as he pressed the gas pedal to the floor.

MOLLY COULD HEAR Mark calling her name, and she wanted desperately to answer him. But she had already dropped the phone when the bedroom door came flying open. She had only seconds to react.

Lips pressed together, she threw herself to the floor on the other side of the bed, thankful that she hadn't turned on the light. That was the good news. The bad news was that she had already changed into her nightgown, and she felt so naked and defenseless under the thin cotton fabric that she wanted to sob and curl into a ball. Only, she knew both of those reactions would likely be fatal.

So she willed herself to steadiness as she crouched on the floor, trying to figure out what to do. Over the blood roaring in her ears, she could hear the sound of someone breathing heavily. The raspy breath brought a mental picture of a barrel-chested man standing on the other side of the room, blocking the doorway. A big man.

Her hands squeezed so tightly that she felt her nails digging into the flesh of her palms.

Mark had said he was on the way. He had said it wouldn't be long. Her job was to stay alive. But how, if this guy had come to kill her? She wondered if he had a gun and if he even knew she was hiding in this room.

Keeping her own breath shallow, she tried to figure out what to do. Mentally, she pictured the floor in the area where she crouched. She'd left her sandals beside the bed, but they'd hardly do as a weapon.

Then she remembered that she'd been hemming a pair of slacks and she hadn't put away her sewing box.

IF A COP stopped him, he'd keep going and lead the guy to Molly's house, Mark thought as he pressed the accelerator to the floor. Of course, if the cop was either Hammer or Daniels, that might not be such a great idea.

He slowed to take a corner, then barreled down Molly's street. Pulling into her driveway, he cut the engine and leaped out of the car. As he charged toward the kitchen door, he saw that it was open, and he swore. She was right. Somebody was here—unless she had laid a trap for *him.*

He didn't want to think that could be true. She'd sounded panicked when she'd called. But after his encounter with Oliver, it was impossible to discount the possibility. He tried to wipe his suspicions out of his mind. Still, he slowed his pace, moving cautiously through the door and into the kitchen. The room was empty. He stood very still, listening. For endless seconds he detected nothing. Then, from the second floor, he heard footsteps crossing the floor. Footsteps that were much too heavy for a small woman like Molly. Footsteps that sounded like a predator on the prowl.

He cursed under his breath, repressing the urge to call out her name as he headed for the stairs. She was in trouble up there, he had no doubt of that now.

Again, he had to stifle his natural impulse to pound up the steps. Instead, he moved cautiously upward, his body bent to make himself less of a target in case someone was waiting for him there.

MOLLY WAS RUMMAGING inside her sewing box for her scissors when she heard the man coming toward her.

Her fingers closed around the twin handles just as the intruder reached her side of the bed and bent to grab her, his hands landing on the straps of her gown.

She thrust her arms up, warding off the attack with her left hand while she jabbed at him with the scissors. It connected with some part of his midsection, and she heard him make a low, dangerous sound.

"You bitch!"

His fingers clutched her straps as he reared back, ripping the thin fabric.

She tried to ignore the sensation of cold air on her breasts as she raised the scissors for another thrust. Her attacker grabbed her arm with one hand. With the other, he slapped her hard across the face before wrenching the scissors away and swinging the weapon at her, as she had swung it at him. Ducking quickly, she felt the blade part her hair, just before she heard someone else surge into the room.

"Mark, watch out. He's got my scissors," she screamed.

Her rescuer made a savage sound as he threw himself on the man, pulling him away from her. They both landed on the bed, rolling and slugging at each other in the dark. She pushed herself up, holding up the front of her gown with one hand and scrambling to find another weapon. The iron cat she used as a doorstop would do, she decided. Rounding the bed again, she tried to get in a blow on the other guy's head. But he wasn't still long enough for her to connect with any part of his anatomy without getting Mark instead.

She heard a curse in response to a punch from Mark. Another punch had the man grunting as he wrenched free and dragged himself to her side of the bed, sliding his body along the wall.

She backed away, giving Mark room. It looked as if he had the guy cornered. Probably Mark thought so, too, until the man flung himself sideways across the bed and onto the other side. Seconds later he was standing on the floor and heading for the door. By the time Mark had reversed his position, the assailant had dashed down the stairs. When Mark tried to follow, she grabbed his shoulder.

"No. You can't catch him."

He spat out a curse, then went absolutely still as he saw her torn nightgown in the light from the hall. She saw the shock on his face. "Oh Lord, Molly. What happened?"

She tried to tug at the gown, thinking she should be embarrassed by her near nudity. But with him, she wasn't. She was only trying to cover herself as a kind of automatic reaction.

"You don't have to feel embarrassed with me." He stopped her from tugging at the gown by reaching out and pulling her into his arms.

A small sound welled in her throat as she melted into his embrace. Her head dropped to his shoulder, and she clung to him, feeling her body begin to shake. The danger was over, and now the reaction had set in.

"Molly, tell me what happened," he demanded. "Did he try to rape you?"

She shook her head quickly, because she didn't want him to think the attack had been sexual. "No. Nothing like that. He just tore my gown because he grabbed the strap."

"You called me when he broke in."

"Yes. I heard him in the house. I did what you said. I locked myself in the bedroom," she explained, her voice becoming stronger as she spoke.

"And he broke in," Mark added, his hands soothing over her shoulders. "Then what?"

"I was hiding on the floor on the other side of the bed. My sewing box was there and I took out the scissors. I cut him, but obviously not enough."

"No. You're lucky. If you'd killed him, they could have gotten you for murder."

"But it was clearly self-defense."

"Mike Randall didn't murder his wife, and they got *him* for murder."

She nodded, then muttered, "I hope I hurt him good. I hope he's got a scissors tattoo on his fat stomach."

"Yeah." Mark gave a short laugh. She joined him, both of them relieving some of their tension.

Mark sobered first. "Do you know why he was here?"

"No." She raised her head, her eyes searching his. "Do you believe me?"

"Yes," he answered, but she couldn't be sure it was the truth, not after the way he'd walked out on her at lunch.

Perhaps it was that memory that made her ask, "Are you thinking that I staged an emergency exclusively for your benefit? That would be the perfect way to get you to trust me, wouldn't it?"

Chapter Eleven

He knew she was waiting for his answer, and there was only one reply he could give. Not just intellectually, but emotionally. The thought of what had almost happened tonight had shaken him to the core. As he held her in his arms, he was profoundly grateful that she'd called him—and that she was unharmed. "No!" he answered in a thick voice. "I think I got here in time to keep something bad from happening."

She was staring up at him, and it was the most natural thing in the world to lower his mouth to hers and tell her how thankful he was that he had arrived in time.

Their lips touched, held. He had meant only to express his relief, but one taste of her, and he was lost. He angled his head, intent on getting more of her, and her quick indrawn breath told him she was just as eager as he for the contact.

If she had stopped him, he would have made himself pull back. But her hands flattened against his back, pressing, stroking, urging him closer. He obliged by pulling her more tightly to him, even as the taste of her, the scent, the intensity of his need swamped him.

His desire for her had started out as lust, but it had

changed into something far more profound. He couldn't name the emotions he felt now. Or perhaps he was afraid to name them. He didn't want to need her. He didn't want to lose control. But he felt it slipping from him.

"Molly." He lifted his mouth enough to whisper her name, just a puff of breath against her lips. She seemed to drink in the syllables and gave them back to him, only now it was his name on her lips.

The brief exchange was like a pledge, he thought in some dim recess of his mind. But conscious thought was rapidly fading away. The only thing he knew was that he had waited so long for her, and she was finally in his arms. In a dark, private bedroom where no one was going to stop them from doing anything they wanted. He angled her away from him, sweeping down the loosened bodice of her gown so that his hand could cup her breasts, stroke over them, find the hardened nipples with his fingers.

She made an incoherent sound and pressed herself into his hands. He felt her skin heat, felt his own body temperature rising.

She was his now. Giving herself to him without reservation. He accepted that gift, praying that he could return it to her in kind. It had been so long since he had made love. And now that Molly was in his arms he was humbled and a little afraid.

He felt his body trembling as he took a step back, easing the two of them toward the bed. His breath was ragged now, and he knew that waiting for fulfillment had become impossible. He must have her now.

But as he steered her across the room, his foot came down on something hard, and he stopped with a jerk.

Looking down, he saw the shiny blades of a scissors, and he cursed.

When he tried to pull away, her arms tightened around him. "Mark, please. Don't stop this time."

He lifted his head and stared down into her passion-drugged eyes, and he knew at that moment he could take anything from her that he wanted. But he also knew that making love with her here and now would be the worst kind of betrayal.

"We can't," he managed to say, hearing the thick, gritty quality of his voice.

"You don't want me?" she asked, her voice barely above a whisper.

"Of course I want you! But the last time I looked, your kitchen door was open. Now a big guy with a scissors wound is outside in the darkness. I know we think he drove away, but he could have come back."

She drew in a quick breath, her eyes going from soft and unfocused to alarmed. "I wasn't thinking about that. I was only thinking about making love with you."

He cupped his hands over her shoulders.

"That's all I was thinking about, too. But the danger has finally filtered into my brain. We have to get out of here. For all I know, he could be coming back with reinforcements."

"Oh, Lord," she said.

"Get dressed." As he spoke, he reached to pull up the bodice of her gown, noting in some corner of his brain that his hands weren't quite steady. For a second she covered his fingers with hers. Then she grabbed the fine fabric and stepped away from him. He stood beside the bed, feeling as though he were in the grips of a dream that was part heaven and part hell. But this was no dream, and he shook his head to clear it. He needed to think, to make plans that went beyond seducing the woman he'd been wanting for as long as he could remember.

She was back in what seemed like moments, wearing a pair of light slacks and a knit shirt.

"Pack your toilet articles and a couple changes of clothing," he told her.

"Why?"

"Because you can't stay here." He ran a hand through his hair. "Someone tried to hurt you. I'm not going to let it happen."

She looked at him with large, questioning eyes. "Mark, what's happening? What's going on?"

"Either someone's after you or they know you're mixed up with me."

"And what are you doing in Perry's Cove?"

"I'm not going to talk about that now. We don't have time for a long explanation. We have to get out of here."

"But you just expect me to go with you? Isn't that taking a pretty big chance?"

"It's taking more of a chance staying in your house. Is there someone you can go to? Someone out of town, because I wouldn't trust anybody around here. Especially not Dean Hammer."

"I never trusted him."

"And not your old friends from the antique gallery."

He watched her process the information, watched her silent debate. "Okay. For now I'll play by your rules."

He released the breath he'd been holding. He was sure that if he told her who he was now, she would never come with him. But he didn't want her going to someone out of town. He wanted to keep her with him, and he knew his reasons weren't entirely honorable. "Then get ready as quickly as you can."

She did as he asked, disappearing into the bathroom to gather up her toothbrush and other essentials. Then she opened dresser drawers, getting out comfortable clothing. A few minutes later she was following him downstairs. She paused when she saw the open door.

"I guess it won't do much good to lock it."

"Do it, if it makes you feel better."

"You said not to trust Hammer. You're saying I shouldn't call the police?" she asked in a voice that had turned unsteady.

"I wouldn't."

She answered with a tight nod, then took a step into the living room and stopped short. Hurrying to the credenza, she ran her hand over the top. Then she looked in back and inspected the floor at the front and sides.

"What are you looking for?" Mark asked her.

"The box is missing!"

He stared at her. "The puzzle box?"

"Yes."

"What else?"

She switched on the light, glancing around the room. When she raised her head to him, her face was strained. "Just the puzzle box."

"What's so important about that damn thing?"

"I don't know! I mean, it was one of the last things Phil gave me, so it was valuable to me for that. But I don't know why someone else would single it out."

"What's in it?" Mark demanded.

"If I knew, I'd tell you."

"Would you?"

"Yes." Her face turned hard as she searched his eyes. "It always comes back to the same thing, doesn't it? You can't force yourself to trust me. Oh, you try. And maybe it lasts for five minutes." She made a snorting sound. "But then you go back to your old way of thinking."

He spread his hands, trying to make her understand, even as he strove to contain his frustration. "I came here thinking there was too much at stake to trust anyone. I didn't count on getting tangled up with you."

"That's an interesting way to put it."

"I'm sorry."

"And why should I trust *you?*"

"Maybe you shouldn't."

She made an exasperated sound. "We should leave. So where are we going?"

She had called a truce. He wasn't going to break it now.

"I was thinking about taking you to my room at the East Point Lodge. Then I figured that might not be any safer than your house."

"You have a better suggestion?"

"I was hoping you would. Are there any vacant properties where we could camp out?"

He watched her think about that for a moment. Really, he loved the serious look on her face when she was grappling with a problem—as long as it wasn't the issue of trust.

"I can do better than that," she finally said. "Our company handles time-share condos in Perry's Landing. I can see which of them are free."

"Okay. Good."

She started for the door, and he put his hand on her

shoulder. ''Wait a minute. Let me go first and make sure it's safe.'' He felt her stiffen, and he was sorry he had to frighten her. But better safe than sorry. Stepping outside, he scanned the area in front of the house and around the side, but saw no one. That didn't mean someone wasn't hiding in the bushes. Returning to the door, he told her to give him another thirty seconds, then hurried to the car, where he opened the passenger door before motioning for her to follow him.

As soon as she jumped in and closed her door, he pulled out of the driveway before she had a chance to fasten her seat belt.

When they were away from the house, he slowed to a normal speed. From the corner of his eye he watched her buckle her seat belt and cast him several sideways glances, but she said nothing.

She was probably wondering why she was willing to trust him—if she was an honest citizen caught in some plot she didn't understand. Despite their unspoken truce, he was grappling with his own uncertainties. In his heart, he wanted to believe in her. He was ninety-five percent sure that she was mystified by what was going on. But he couldn't dismiss that five percent of doubt—because it could get him killed. He tried to keep those thoughts off his face as he drove toward the real estate office. When they reached the building, it was not quite dawn, but there was already a car in the parking lot.

His mind jumped back to the previous hour. They'd been together almost all the time, but he'd left her alone while he'd gone out to check on the exterior.

Could she have made a phone call to someone and said where they were going? He didn't think there had been time. And if she had called, it wouldn't do much good to ask. Instead, he said, "Who the hell is here at this hour?"

She glanced at him, probably reacting to the sharp tone of his voice. Then she studied the car. "Doris Masters."

Molly had mentioned her before, he remembered. "What is she, a workaholic? Does she usually come in so early?"

"I don't know. I don't keep track of her movements. And *I'm* not usually here this early, so I can't really answer your question."

"Right. Well, make sure she can't figure out where we're going."

She gave him a tight nod and started to exit the car. He put a hand on her shoulder. "I'll come with you."

"Why?"

"I don't like leaving you alone."

"Or you're interested in what I have to say to Doris."

He didn't bother to answer, only followed her to the door. It was locked, and she searched through her purse for a key before they could enter.

Inside, most of the lights were off in the front, but he could see illumination coming from down the hall. Moments after they walked in, a blond-haired woman hurried into the reception area, her expression registering alarm.

"Who's there?" she asked, then stopped short when she saw who had come into the office.

"Oh, it's you," she said, addressing Molly. "You gave me a start. I wasn't expecting anyone so early."

Molly gestured toward him. "Mar— Mr. Ramsey and I had arranged to start early."

"I see," the woman answered.

''Mark Ramsey, Doris Masters,'' Molly said.

''Nice to meet you,'' he said automatically, his gaze squarely on the other real estate agent. She was staring at him, just as he was staring at her. The moment he'd set eyes on her, he'd known she was the woman making love with Oliver Garrison at the antique mall. Only, they hadn't done the dirty deed because Garrison had answered a phone call, and she'd rushed out, intent on some urgent mission.

The way she was focused on him made his flesh crawl. What? Did she know he'd been outside in the dark, watching her and Garrison? Did she know about the recent break-in at Molly's house and the subsequent fight between the intruder and Mark Ramsey? Was that why she was at work so early?

There was no way to answer any of those questions now. But he was pretty sure that finding her here at this hour of the morning was significant. She turned to Molly, her voice pleasant and even. It was low for a woman, and the effect was a little jarring. ''Can I help you with something?''

''No. You don't have to bother,'' Mark answered for Molly. ''But I would like *your* opinion on the rental market in Perry's Cove.''

''Isn't Mrs. Dumont helping you?'' she asked, her voice sharpening. ''When you start with one agent, you're supposed to stick with her.''

''Of course, but it's always good to get another opinion.''

Molly took her cue, slipping into the back of the building while Mark kept Doris engaged. The woman flicked a glance over her shoulder, looking as if she wanted to follow Molly. But there was no way to do that without ignoring Mark's direct question.

He saw her take a breath as she turned back to him. "What do you want to know?" she asked.

"What would you rent if you were new in town?" he asked.

She stared off into the distance for a moment. "It depends on your price range."

"Would you say that property here is more expensive than in other areas?" he asked, the question coming off the top of his head. He wasn't anywhere near as interested in the answer as he was in the woman. He'd been distracted the last time he'd seen her. Now that he was face-to-face with her, the husky quality of her voice teased him, and her features twanged at some memory chord that he couldn't catch onto. He studied her face. It was generally rounded, with her nose a bit sharp and her eyes wide set. They were brown. And somehow he thought they would look more natural blue. But he couldn't say why.

She was staring at him with the same intensity—probably because she'd gotten a call from Oliver or the goon who had broken into Molly's house. Mark wanted to turn away, but he stayed where he was, knowing he had to keep the enemy occupied so that Molly could do her work.

"I'd say the prices in Perry's Cove are steep, compared to other areas," she said. For a moment he didn't know why she had made the observation. Then he remembered that he had asked her a question and she was answering.

"So where's a good area to try?"

She sighed. "Well, development is pushing north and south of town. The newer properties are always the most expensive. So I'd look for something that was built at least fifteen years ago. That will be the best value.'' She ended the little essay, then asked a question of her own. ''How long are you planning to stay in town?''

''A few months.'' Mark shoved his hand into his pocket. He hardly knew this woman, but his strongest impression was that he didn't like her. He had the feeling that the animosity was mutual, and she was struggling to hide the reaction.

''All set,'' Molly said as she came back.

''So where are you headed?'' Doris asked.

''North,'' Molly said.

''If I need to get in touch with you, where should I call?'' Doris pressed.

''I'll check in later,'' Molly said.

Mark saw Doris shoot her a nasty look. Probably Molly caught it too, but she acted as if she didn't notice a thing. When they exited the building, he murmured, ''You handled that exactly right.''

''Thanks.''

''She won't be able to go back into the files and figure out where we're going?'' he asked as they climbed into his car.

''I don't think so. I took a duplicate key. I didn't record the information. And I erased the computer record of what I checked.''

''Very thorough.''

''I feel like a spy.''

He started the engine and looked at her. ''I take it we're not going north?''

She gave a small laugh. ''Well, actually, we are. I was thinking that she'd figure I was lying, so I told her the truth.''

He joined in the laughter. ''Nicely convoluted.''

"Thanks. I think." She swallowed. "I take it you think she's mixed up in this."

"Yeah, I think so. I think Oliver Garrison is mixed up in it. And the two of them were...acting pretty friendly tonight at the antique gallery."

Her gaze shot to him. "You're saying you saw them?"

"Right. They were interrupted by a phone call. It could have something to do with earlier this evening—actually, last night—when I went back to the house where we found the boxes. They were gone, but someone jumped me when I came back outside."

She was taking it all in. "You're saying you went back to that house where we were yesterday and somebody attacked you?" she asked carefully, sounding genuinely shocked by the revelations. Unless she was a very good actress. He canceled that thought as soon as it surfaced. He had to stop thinking about her that way—starting now.

He looked over and saw her watching him. "Do you need to stop by your hotel room and get your stuff?"

"I don't want us going anywhere we might be expected."

"You're keeping your room?" she asked.

"Uh-huh."

"Isn't that expensive?"

"I like the expense better than the alternative."

"Yes," he heard her murmur.

"How far north are we going?" he asked.

"About five miles." She gave him the address.

He nodded and kept his gaze on the road. He'd been holding out on Molly all this time, and he'd come up with one rationale after another for his behavior. Now he knew he had to level with her. But he was sure he wasn't going to like her reaction to his duplicity, so he kept driving.

"Do you need me to tell you where to turn?" she asked, interrupting his thoughts.

"No."

At her inquisitive look, he added, "I told you I'd been in town before."

"Okay," she answered, and he knew she was waiting for him to say more.

"We'll talk when we get there," he muttered.

"Okay."

She was keeping her responses clipped.

He felt his stomach knot as he pictured her explosion of outrage when he delivered his bombshell. He found the street address and located the building with only a little trouble, then scanned the parking lot of the time-share complex before deciding it was safe to get out. Dawn was imminent, and he wanted to use the last bit of darkness to hide them.

"Let's go. Just in case someone's up, walk fast, but don't look like you're hiding from anyone," he ordered as he opened the back door and collected his mask case from the back seat.

"I'll try to reconcile those two goals," she answered dryly as she picked up her own carryall.

"This isn't a game," he snapped, then tried to make amends by reaching over and covering one of her hands with his. "Sorry, I'm kind of on edge."

"I understand," she murmured, although he knew she didn't really have the whole picture. Not yet. But the bombshell was going to hit her soon.

She led the way to the second-floor apartment.

Inside, when she started to turn on a light, he stopped her hand. "We should close the drapes first."

"Right."

They both walked around the apartment, blocking off the view, giving him another chance to stall, he thought as he surveyed their home away from home. It was a nice place, with two bedrooms, a great room and a modern kitchen. Molly had one of the cabinets open, he saw when he met up with her there. Her back to him, she was checking out basic cooking supplies and had just set a bottle of olive oil on the counter.

He could see the tension in her shoulders. Probably she didn't like being cooped up here with him.

"This place comes with food?" he asked, just to have something to say.

"I guess people buy stuff and can't use it up. So they leave it for the next guests," she replied without turning.

"Right. Makes sense," he answered, knowing how inane he sounded. All he could think was that he'd waited too long to talk to her, and now he knew that whatever he said was going to come off wrong.

She turned, and the expression on her face made his breath still in his chest.

"Mark," she said.

Somehow he managed to dredge up enough voice to say, "I have to talk to you."

"I think it better wait till later."

"There's stuff you don't know about me. Stuff I have to tell you."

She stopped short, three feet from him, and his heart began to pound.

Chapter Twelve

"I've been thinking that you have your reasons for not talking about why you came to Perry's Cove," Molly said.

"Yeah," Mark managed.

"I made an issue of your telling me what you were doing here, but right now I don't care. What I care about is that we're together—alone."

"Maybe you should be afraid of that."

She raised her chin slightly, gave him a direct look. "Maybe I should be afraid of you but I'm not. I'm trying to think logically, and I think your actions speak louder than words. You saved my life last night. You probably saved my life when that bucket of shingles fell off the roof, and you risked your own life both times."

He couldn't answer. All he could do was watch her close the distance between them. She stopped so close to him that he could feel her warm, moist breath fanning his neck. The warmth spread over his skin, through his body, turning to fire in his veins. For an eternity Molly didn't move, and he felt anticipation and need well up inside him. It seemed as if he'd wanted her all his adult life, and now he simply had to reach for her. But at that moment in time he was powerless to ask for what he wanted because he knew in his soul that he couldn't be the one to make demands.

Still, demands clamored inside him like a wild animal clawing its way through raw flesh.

When she brought her lips to his, he made a low, anguished sound in his throat. He should put his hands on her shoulders and set her away from him. He should tell her who and what he was before they went any farther. But he was helpless to do anything besides wrap his arms around her and drag her to him.

He felt an almost physical rush of blood from his brain to the lower part of his body. Gathering her to him, he kissed her with a kind of desperation that he might have meant as a warning, because that was the only warning he was capable of giving.

He plundered her mouth, feasted on her, absorbed her sweetness. She tasted of sun and ocean breezes and all things good, all things free. All the things he had missed during the years when he had been locked away from the world. He had thought he knew what he wanted then. He realized now that his fantasies had been nothing compared to the reality of this woman's kiss.

When the kiss broke, he dragged in a ragged breath. Unconsciously, he had squeezed his eyes tightly closed.

"You don't want a man as needy as I am," he muttered.

"Mark Ramsey, you don't know yourself, do you? I can tell how much you want me. But awhile ago, you stopped us from making love because you knew we had to leave my house. You keep doing the right thing. The honorable thing."

He made a strangled sound then, because she had spoken part of the truth—but only part. He wanted her so badly he ached, yet he *was* trying to do the honorable thing. She had called him by the name he'd given her—Mark Ramsey. He barely knew who that man was supposed to be. And what he did know, he didn't like.

He wanted to tell her about it. But the words wouldn't come, not when he felt the gentle touch of her fingers on his face. His altered face. She traced the line of his cheekbone, the ridge of flesh below his nose, the sandpaper of his day's growth of beard.

He played a game with himself then. A mental game. If she felt the well-hidden scars, he would tell her who he was. But she apparently felt nothing, besides his heated flesh.

Her finger returned to his lips, retracing territory she had claimed with her mouth.

He felt her hand shake and knew that she wasn't quite as confident as she appeared. She'd told him she hadn't been with anyone since her husband's suicide. He was sure he could stop her now with the right words, but he didn't have the will. Not when her trembling finger slipped between his lips, playing with the sensitive inner flesh, then dragged across his teeth. He snatched her hand away, not because he didn't like what she was doing. He liked it too much, and he wanted more.

Yet at the same time some part of his fevered brain warned him to be careful with her. She might want to prove that she trusted him. But she was fragile—probably more fragile than she realized.

He bent to kiss her eyebrows, the tender place

where her hair met her cheek. His lips flirted with her eyelashes before coming gently back to her mouth.

He didn't want to hurt her. He wanted to give her pleasure. He wanted to make her passion match his. But he was badly out of practice. He'd lived in his fantasies for a long time, and fantasy sex was a lot different from the real thing—easier, under his complete control. In a fantasy, there was no problem about pleasing your partner. She was there to do your bidding, to fulfill your every whim.

Her hands were restless, stroking his back and shoulders, her touch exciting and inciting him, yet still he stood where he was because he wasn't quite sure what to do next.

"Bedroom," she murmured as though she somehow knew that she had to take over the role of leader, at least for now.

It flashed through his mind to tell her that she didn't want to be with a man who had spent the past five years in prison. Instead, what came to his lips was, "Yes."

She reached for his hand, and he knit his fingers with hers, holding tight as they made their way down the darkened hallway to what was probably the master suite. He had come in here before when he'd closed the blinds, but he'd been too preoccupied to pay much attention to the room. It was like that now. He got a quick impression of a queen-size bed before the feel of her fingers on his chest burned their way through the fabric of his shirt.

Slowly, then more quickly, she began sliding the buttons open. He heard a rush of breath in his lungs. She opened the shirt, pushing it off his shoulders as she bent to press her cheek against his chest then turned her head to give him an openmouthed kiss.

"Oh, Molly," he gasped.

She pulled back a little, staring at one of the bruises on his chest from the pummeling he'd gotten the night before. "You—"

"Just kiss it and make it well."

She did, gently, tenderly.

His hands came up to clasp her with equal tenderness, as though she were the most precious thing in the world. And she was. In his dreams, he had compelled her to come to him. She had had no choice but to bend to his will. But now she had a choice, and what she chose to do was sweep his shirt off his shoulders and provoke him with her clever mouth.

He stood there in the center of the room, naked to the waist, more needy and aroused than he had ever been in his life. When she took a step back, he groaned in protest. But she wasn't going far, he quickly discovered. She pulled her knit top over her head, and he had only a few seconds to appreciate that view before she was reaching for the catch of her bra and sending the garment to join the shirts lying on the floor.

He stared at her, dazed. Of course he had imagined her breasts. In his male chauvinist fantasy he had made them very generous and jutting with large coral-colored nipples. As he looked at her now, the image seemed startlingly wrong. She was much more delicately made, small and gently rounded with beautiful pink nipples that beaded toward him, proclaiming her arousal.

Still, her face told him that she was worried about his reaction to her body, to the bold step she had just taken.

"You are so very beautiful. Perfect for me," he said, reaching toward her, cupping one soft mound in his hand, then gently circling her hardened nipple with his forefinger.

"Oh, Mark."

He reached for her then, drawing her into his arms, desperate for the feel of her breasts against his chest. A shuddering sigh escaped from her lips as he clasped her to him.

He felt her vulnerability, and his own. And this time when he kissed her, it was with a gentle possessiveness that was no less urgent than the whirlwind of passion he had felt before.

His hands moved over her naked back, down her ribs, and she did the same, touching him, stroking him, sending little currents of sensation through his body even as she made small, incoherent sounds that told him how much she liked his touch.

The only thought in his mind was that he needed to get closer to her—as close as he could get. When he eased away so that he could reach for the button at the top of her slacks, she let him do what he wanted, and followed his example, her fingers fumbling with the snap at his waistband.

As her hand slid his zipper down, he went very still, the sensation of her palm pressing against his erection taking his breath away.

She kicked away her slacks. He did the same.

She laid her head against his shoulder, then turned her face so that she could brush her lips against the hot flesh just under his jaw, the gesture so unconsciously erotic that he felt his knees buckle.

Before he lost the ability to stand, he brought her

down to the surface of the bed, then caught her hand when she tried to touch him intimately.

"I'm too close to the edge," he muttered, gathering her in his arms, rocking her against him, then bending to press his face against her breasts.

With her hands she cradled the back of his head as he took one taut nipple into his mouth, hungry for the taste of her and hungry to feed her arousal. When she cried out at the wet, tugging pressure, he felt a wave of gratification that staggered him.

He slid his hand down her flank, stroking her hip and then pressing his palm to the springy hair at the juncture of her legs, and was rewarded with her low sound of pleasure.

He slid his fingers lower, dipping into her moist warmth, parting her delicate folds so that he could stroke her.

She moved against his hand, her breath accelerating before she moaned out a plea. "Mark, don't make me wait."

"I want you as ready for this as I am."

"I am!" She opened her mouth against his shoulder, her teeth worrying his hot flesh. "Please, you're pushing me over the edge, and I want you inside me when you do."

He wanted that, too. Gently he eased her to her back. Shifting above her, he moved between her legs, then took her in one sure, gratifying stroke, burying his body in the warm clasp of hers.

She slid her arms around him, held him tightly. Moving her hips, she took him deeper inside her, silently asking for more.

In the long years of exile, he had thought only of

physical fulfillment. But the power of the moment stunned him.

He raised his head, looking down at her, seeing the passion and the wonder on her face. When he pulled back and then came forward in a deep, claiming stroke, she touched her fingers to his lips, his face.

He wanted this first time of loving with her to last. He wanted to create a memory that the two of them would share down their long years together. Their first time. But the need of his body was too great. Quickly the pace became more urgent, more demanding.

Great waves of pleasure washed over him in time to the rhythm of his body surging into hers.

"Molly."

"I'm...with you. I'm with you...all the way," she gasped out between broken breaths, meeting each thrust and retreat with the motion of her hips.

He was on the edge, desperate to bring her satisfaction before his body demanded fulfillment. Then he spun out of control in a tight spiral of urgent need that shattered in a burst of pleasure so intense that he cried out in wonder.

He thought he had forged ahead too quickly, and knew a surge of regret. Then he felt her nails digging into the slick flesh of his shoulders, felt her body convulsing under him, around him.

When the storm had swept past, he shifted his weight off her, taking her with him, holding her in his arms.

"Thank you," he said, his voice hoarse with emotion.

"Thank *you.*"

He held on to her, unable to break the connection.

He knew they had done this in the wrong order.

There was so much he needed to say to her. He had to tell her who he was and why he had come to Perry's Cove. But he was too wrung out, physically and emotionally. And when she snuggled down against him, he felt himself drifting off to sleep, thankful that the dark curtains blocked the morning light.

He woke once, glad of her warmth beside him. She murmured something he didn't catch before snuggling back against him.

The next time he woke, she wasn't there. When he realized he was alone, he felt a prickle of uneasiness skitter over his skin.

"Molly?"

She didn't answer, and his gaze flicked to the bathroom door. It was open and the room beyond was dark. She wasn't in there, either.

Sitting up, he glanced across the floor. Her clothing was missing, but his was still scattered where he'd left it.

Had she gone out?

His heart was pounding as he pulled on his slacks. Barefoot and shirtless, he hurried down the hall.

Relief washed over him when he saw Molly, dressed in her clothing of the night before, standing beside the dining-room table where they'd dumped their luggage. Then he realized what she was doing. She had opened the case with his mask—the case he had forgotten to relock—and had reached inside. As he watched, she held up the mast and looked at it, her face contorting as she smoothed out the ripples in the rubber.

"What are you doing?" he demanded.

She jumped and spun to face him, the mask still in her hands. "What the hell is this?" she asked.

"What the hell are you doing poking through my stuff?" he countered.

"I was looking for some clean clothing for you."

"So you opened the case," he snapped, defensiveness making his voice more harsh than he intended.

"It felt light, like it didn't have anything in it. I wondered why you'd brought it." She sighed. "But you're right, I shouldn't have been prying. Unfortunately, I did," she added, her voice turning sharp and edgy. "And now I want to know what kind of sick game you're playing with me." She gestured toward the mask. "It's hard to get a fix on this thing in its current form. But it's Mike Randall's face, isn't it?"

"Yes. I was going to tell you. I was going to tell you as soon as we got here."

Her eyes flashed. "You were never going to tell me what you're up to."

"We need to talk," he answered, his voice going from gritty to raw.

She gave a sharp laugh, her eyes challenging him as she put the mask back in the case, then sat in one of the large wicker chairs.

He felt too restless to stay still, but he forced himself to sit in the chair opposite her.

He wasn't sure how to say what he knew he had to tell her. So he started with ground they'd trod before. "Like most people in town suspect, I came to Perry's Cove to investigate the Mike Randall case."

"Well, you denied that to me once. Are we making progress?"

He ignored her sarcastic tone and said, "Somebody in town wanted it to look like he killed his wife. And they did a good job. He was convicted of the crime and sent to prison—where he might have sat and rotted for the rest of his miserable life. Then he read an article about the Light Street Foundation. They offer various charitable services, and they'd just started a program to reexamine the evidence in cases with merit. Mike Randall wrote them a letter, laying out the facts of his case. He was lucky that they took him on."

"And you work for the Light Street Foundation?" Molly supplied. "But why did you bring a mask of Mike's face?"

"It's hard to explain. Let me work my way up to it."

She gave him a tight nod, and he saw that her hands were gripping the arms of her chair. He was just as tense as she was. In fact, it had become impossible for him to sit still, so he heaved himself out of the chair, paced toward the window and slid the curtains aside so he could look out briefly before turning back to her.

"Mike Randall wanted to find out who railroaded him into prison. So he came up with a plan to poke around in Perry's Cove. See, for one thing, he had a fair amount of money at his disposal. The Light Street Foundation makes a hundred-thousand-dollar cash payment to the people they prove innocent."

"That's pretty generous of them."

"Yeah. It's to help them get back on their feet. Probably you could have used something like that after your husband's death."

"Yes," she murmured. Then, "You're getting off the subject."

"Right. Mike had another source of money, too. There was a million-dollar policy taken out on his wife's life. A policy he didn't know about until after she was killed. But he was the beneficiary. It was bought only a couple of months before her death, which was one of the pieces of evidence the prosecutors used to convict him.''

Molly nodded.

''After he was convicted of her murder, he forfeited the money, of course. But when he was exonerated, they had to pay out.''

''A million dollars,'' Molly whispered.

''Yeah. With five years of interest, actually. The Light Street Foundation got them to pay that, too.''

''A lot of money.''

''Right. So Mike Randall had plenty of cash to play with. He decided to be really clever.'' He swallowed, then went on rapidly while he could force himself to say what he had to.

''He had plastic surgery on his face to make him look different, and he bought a new identity,'' he said, letting those facts sink in. She stared at him, and he knew the exact moment when she put the pieces together.

''You...'' Her voice trailed off in a kind of incredulous wheeze. She looked as if a bomb had gone off next to her. Every rigid line of her face silently begged him to say it wasn't true.

He ached to oblige her. He ached to take it all back, to tell her he had simply been making up a story. But neither one of them would have believed that now.

Swallowing around the boulder in his throat, he said, ''Yes. I used to be Mike Randall.''

She sat there like a doll with the stuffing shaken out of her. But her eyes moved. Her gaze slid over his face, his body.

''I kept trying to figure out why I thought I knew you. But you're different. Not just your face.''

''Yeah.'' He didn't feel any better than he had a

few moments ago. But at least now the lie was out in the open. "One of my chief recreational activities in prison was pumping iron. I acquired some new muscles. And my voice is different, too, courtesy of a fellow inmate who slammed his fist into my throat."

"Oh." For a moment she looked sorry that he'd been injured. But almost instantly her features hardened again. "So you've been playing games with me since you got here. Like that bull about how you came here before and saw me."

"That wasn't bull. I *was* here before and I did see you. And I was attracted to you. You must have known that. You must have known that I wanted you from the moment I saw you. Don't *you* lie and deny it."

He was sorry as soon as he'd said the last part. He had no right to push her on anything. He wanted to go to her, hold her, make her feel the incredible connection between them.

She had opened her mouth to say something he doubtless didn't want to hear.

Before she could speak, he hurried on, trying to soften the harsh words. "You were attracted to me, too, in the old days. But neither one of us would have done anything about it back then because we were both married. Both trapped in bad marriages. At least I know mine was. And from what you've told me, life with Phil wasn't a picnic. But I'm not going to rationalize my feelings for you back then or my feelings for you now. All I know is that when I was in prison, I spent a lot of time thinking about you. Not some other woman. You."

"Was I your masturbation fantasy?"

"I wouldn't put it that way."

"How would you put it?"

"Thinking about you, maintaining a connection with you, helped me keep my sanity."

She made a snorting noise. "Right. You formed such a deep attachment that when you came back here, you told me right away who you were."

"I couldn't."

She folded her arms across her chest. "What's your rationale for that?"

"I didn't know who was involved in Veronica's murder. For all I knew, you could have been deep into it."

Anger flared in her eyes. "Oh, right. I'm into murder. What was my motive?"

"Look, your husband killed himself. We don't know why. Maybe it had something to do with Veronica."

"Oh, come on. That was two years later."

"So something went wrong."

"I don't have to listen to this."

"No, you don't. But I was hoping you would."

"I was a fool to get so wound up with you," she muttered. Springing out of the chair, she stalked out of the room, and he heard a door slam, then a lock click.

IN THE PARKING LOT of the real estate office, Doris Masters clicked off her cell phone. Reaching up, she began to finger her short blond hair. When she was nervous, she played with it, and this morning she was very nervous. For several heartbeats she sat staring into space. Then, with a scowl on her face, she climbed out of her car and stalked back into the building. Sometimes she wanted to murder Oliver Garrison.

And sometimes she wondered how she had let him trap her in this whole harebrained scheme. A long time ago she'd been so in love with the bastard that she'd let him talk her into a whole bunch of stupid moves. Moves she now regretted. She'd wanted to leave Perry's Cove. He'd wanted her with him. So she'd gone to a lot of pain, trouble and expense to stay here.

That was when she'd been convinced they were going to get rich. Now she was spending a lot of time thinking about how she could get away from him. He was too unpredictable. She'd turned her life upside down for him. But then she'd been sickened as she watched him manipulate people. Like herself, she silently admitted. And Jerry Tilden. Oliver had chosen to work with the man. Now he was getting ready to force him out of the partnership. Did that mean he was planning to kill him? Send him to jail?

Once she'd been in awe of Oliver. Now their relationship was barely tolerable to her—and only when things were going well. She'd honestly thought the bad part was over. But every time she thought she was safe, something else happened to shake up her feeling of complacency. Like Mark Ramsey showing up in Perry's Cove. Mike had sent him on ahead to stir things up. Then he'd showed up, too.

She just wished she knew exactly what their motives were. Revenge, certainly. And maybe blackmail. She shuddered.

Then, with a sigh, she unlocked the door and entered the building.

Inside, she went back to the rental property section. She didn't know where Mike had gone, but it was a sure bet that Mark Ramsey and Molly Dumont were still in town. They had gone somewhere after that thug had broken into her house, and there were only so many places they could be hiding. Her orders from Oliver were to find them, and she didn't like taking orders. But in this case, she understood the urgency. The faster they did something about Mark Ramsey, the better.

The man's face leaped into her mind, and she went very still, mentally studying his features as a sick, unsettled feeling swept over her. The moment she'd gotten close to him, every nerve ending in her body had begun to tingle. There was something so familiar about him that she could almost bring the context to mind. But not quite. So she stopped trying to pull it into focus, thinking that if she didn't dwell on it, it would come to her.

Of course, there were other unknowns, too. Had he and Molly Dumont cooked up something together before he'd come to town? Or had she hooked up with him by accident? Either way, it was too bad for Molly.

Doris was a supremely practical woman. The Mark Ramsey–Molly Dumont puzzle would solve itself eventually. Right now she had to figure out where in the hell they had gone to ground so Oliver's hired thugs could take care of them. Sitting down at the computer, she brought up the file on rental properties and began to search.

IT WAS EVENING AGAIN when Molly uncurled her legs and shifted to her back. She was lying on the bed in the smaller of the condo's two bedrooms. Not the room where she and Mark had made love. The other one.

She'd lain there for a long time because she couldn't

bear to look at the man who was still out there beyond the closed door.

She'd longed for the oblivion of sleep, but sleep had been impossible. She was too keyed up. At first she'd been angry about the way he had treated her. Then she'd been sad. Then she'd been numb. Then she'd been angry again. And the worst part was that he'd fooled her so completely. She'd even wondered if they'd been lovers in a past life. What a joke!

Since Mike Randall had left town, he'd been in her thoughts all too often. She'd had fantasies about him. She'd imagined the two of them together. She'd even thought about writing him in prison.

She sat up and snorted.

Now he was back. And he hadn't trusted her enough to tell her who he was. But he'd taken her to bed.

She stopped herself there, struggling to be fair. That part hadn't exactly been his fault. She'd wanted to make love with him and she'd pushed them into it.

Her hands clenched, and she squeezed her eyes shut as though that could wipe away the pain. She'd fooled herself into thinking that she might have a future with this new man who had come to Perry's Cove. Another sick joke.

Again she told herself to play fair. On an intellectual level she understood why Mike—no, she'd better call him Mark, or she was in danger of betraying him, the way he expected her to do—had been cautious. He had to be cautious.

From his point of view somebody had set him up for murder six years ago. And there was no reason they wouldn't do it again. Or worse. In fact, it was a hundred percent likelihood. They had already pulled off their big play. Now they had to protect their interests. Since Mark Ramsey had come to town asking questions about the old case, he was a logical target. Probably they'd been nervous ever since the conviction had been overturned. Probably they'd been waiting for somebody to show up and try to figure out who they were.

So who *were* they? Her mind tried to shy away from that, too. But grim conclusions kept working their way back into her thoughts. Oliver Garrison. His new girlfriend. Phil. Bill Bauder. Probably the sheriff, too.

She was picturing them making plans together, when the door opened and she looked up. Mark crossed the room, heading for the bed where she sat propped against the pillows.

His voice was a harsh whisper when he said, "Come on. We've got to get out of here. Now."

Chapter Thirteen

''Get your shoes on,'' Mark ordered.

Molly blinked, even as the urgency in his voice propelled her to action. He wasn't here to invite her to tea. He had respected her privacy—until now.

She pulled on her shoes, then raised her questioning gaze to his.

''I was standing by the window looking out at the parking lot. I saw two men get out of a car and head for this building. They don't look like they came here for a beach vacation.''

''How did they find us?''

''I'd like to know,'' he said tightly as he led her out of the bedroom and down the hall to the great room.

''I didn't tell them.''

He uttered a curse. ''I wasn't saying you did.''

The conversation ended abruptly when she heard the rasp of metal against metal. Her gaze flew to the door as she watched the lock turning.

They had the key! But the chain was on the door. That should hold them—for another ten seconds.

Mark hurried her through the dining area, where he picked up the box with his mask and stuffed it into her carryall. They had just stepped into the kitchen when the front door creaked on its hinges. Through the gap where the chain held the door closed, she could see a man's face. He was wearing a mask like a Wild West outlaw's.

"Come on!" Mark growled when he felt Molly hesitate.

"Wait!" She used up precious seconds to pick up the bottle of olive oil she'd left on the counter and hurled it at the door with all her strength. She felt a surge of satisfaction as the man jumped back and the bottle shattered against the hard surface, sending shards of glass and oil flying all over the hall floor.

Mark's hand clasped hers in a death grip. "Out of here! Now!" he urged as he pulled her toward the balcony.

They were two stories up. Did he expect her to jump? She'd never make it.

Still he dragged her along after him, and when she stepped outside into the twilight, she saw that a rope was coiled on the concrete and tied to the metal railing. Apparently, while she'd been brooding in her room Mark had been busy arranging an escape route for the two of them, just in case.

She would have bet that nobody could find them at the condo. Obviously she'd been wrong. Thank God Mark had been prepared for disaster.

He tossed the rope over the side, and she heard the end hit the concrete below.

Concrete. Not a nice soft flower bed.

"Go!" he urged her.

She eyed the rope, thinking that there was no way she could go down that thing. She'd failed every climbing test they'd ever given in high school, and she'd told herself she was never getting near another dangling piece of hemp again.

A groaning noise from the front door told her there was no choice. The chain couldn't hold long.

Gritting her teeth, she climbed over the railing and reached for the rope. She had lowered herself a couple of feet when the front door burst open and two men crashed into the apartment's entryway. Both of them were hiding behind bandanas, and both held guns pointed toward the living area.

If Molly hadn't been gripped by fear, the ensuing scene might have been funny. Like a couple of actors in a bad chase movie, the men went sprawling on the oil-slick tile. Their feet went out from under them, and they landed on their butts on the foyer floor.

Oil splashed on the walls. But oil wasn't the only menace covering the flat surface. The glass was more dangerous.

When the men started yelping in pain, she knew they'd been cut.

''Go!'' Mark growled.

She had no choice. She started slowly down the rope, grateful to discover that Mark had knotted the hemp every foot or so, which gave her a much better grip.

As she lowered herself, she could hear cursing and groaning from the apartment.

When she looked up, she saw that Mark wasn't waiting for the rope. He climbed over the balcony, threw the carryall over the side, then lowered himself with his feet dangling and let go. He whizzed past her, and her heart leaped into her throat. It was all she could do to keep her grip on the rope.

''Jump. Come on. I'll catch you. We have to get

the hell out of here. They're mad as hornets up there,'' Mark hissed.

She was only halfway down, and fear clogged her throat. But she understood that he was right. So she forced her stiff fingers to unhook themselves from the rope.

She came down heavily, landing against Mark's chest, and for a terrifying moment it felt as though she couldn't breathe. He held her to him for pounding heartbeats.

''Are you okay?''

''Yes.''

He bent to pick up the bag, then locked his hand with hers, leading her along the edge of the building, keeping close to the balconies.

''Where the hell are they?'' a frantic voice from above rang out.

''Don't know,'' came the clipped answer.

Apparently the men had been too busy to spot them on the balcony, Molly thought. At least she hoped so as they dashed across the parking lot to Mark's car. He handed her the keys and the carryall.

''Get in the driver's seat,'' he said. ''If there's any trouble, clear out.''

''What about you?''

''I'll be back in five minutes. If I'm not, I'll meet you…'' He paused. ''Where's a good place?''

She thought for several moments. Not her house. Or the real estate office. Or the East Point Lodge. ''The parking lot behind Mario's,'' she finally said, naming an Italian restaurant on the edge of town.

''Got it.''

He was already sprinting away as she started the

engine. She watched him heading for a car parked across from their building.

He ducked inside, and she waited with her heart in her mouth, praying that he would get back to her in time.

Suddenly an explosion sounded and a shot whizzed past the car Mark was in.

She wanted to scream his name, but she kept her lips pressed together as he leaped from the car and took off around the side of the building.

Lord, now what?

Around her, lights were blinking on and she could hear some of the residents of the condo complex talking.

"What was that?"

"A car backfiring."

Yeah, right, she thought. But under the circumstances, she wouldn't have wanted to consider that someone might be firing a gun.

She hunched over the wheel in anxiety, aching to follow Mark. But she had to wait here, since this was where he expected to find her. It seemed like several decades later before Mark appeared, running toward the car.

Before he reached it, a man sprang from the shadows and leaped on him.

She wheeled the car around, heading toward Mark, even as she saw the man take him down to the grass beside the building.

They were in the shadows, but she heard them trading blows. It was Mark who stood up several moments later, the gun in his hand. He scrabbled over the ground, picked up whatever he'd been carrying and ran toward her.

The moment he was in the car, she gunned the engine and roared off.

"Good going," he muttered. He'd turned to the back seat and was putting something in the bag.

"They'll be after us."

"Not likely. I pulled some wires out of their electrical system."

She breathed out a small sigh. "Are you all right?"

He sat forward again. "Yeah."

"What should I do?"

"I'm thinking." She saw his face rigid with concentration. "We got away, but they know my car. And yours. And if we steal one, we'll have Hammer on our tail."

"One of the real estate agents is on vacation. She left her car at the office. I think the keys are in her desk."

"Too dangerous. Doris will spot us."

They had come out onto the highway. Molly headed for town, feeling exposed and vulnerable, even when she knew that the bad guys couldn't be following in the disabled car.

"Turn in here," Mark said suddenly.

She did as he asked, pulling off the highway into an older, working-class neighborhood where the lots were large and weedy and most of the houses were in need of paint.

Mark scanned the properties, then pointed to one that looked particularly disreputable. Trash littered the yard, and several older cars were pulled along the side of the driveway and behind a freestanding garage.

"Maybe one of those," he muttered.

"You want me to stop here?"

"Yes."

She pulled into the driveway and waited nervously while he headed for one of the cars parked on the far side of the garage from the house. When he tried the handle, the door opened.

Mark climbed inside, and she leaned forward, trying to see what he was doing. But all her attention didn't stay focused on him. She kept turning her head in all directions, trying to see if anybody was aware of what was going on. When she saw Mark sprint down the street, she went rigid.

In a moment he was back at the old car, and she heard the engine turn over. He maneuvered the car beside her and rolled down the window.

"Follow me."

His memory of the area was good. He led her to a spot where the roads were little more than tracks through the sand.

He got her to pull in behind a dune and leave his vehicle. Then she climbed into the car he'd liberated. The body was rusted and the upholstery was torn. Hopefully, nobody would be too upset about its disappearance.

Minutes later, after he'd stowed the carryall in the back seat, they were on their way again.

"Where did you learn to hot-wire a car?" she asked.

"From my prison buddies."

She nodded. "And I listened to the discussions about license plates, too. I switched them with a car down the road."

She made a small, distressed noise.

"You don't approve?"

"I guess I don't have a choice."

"We do what we have to," he answered, then

twisted in his seat to look at her. "That was a pretty good trick with the bottle of olive oil. How did you think of that?"

"I don't know. I just saw the bottle and thought it might be a good idea."

"It was. You gave us the extra time we needed."

"Thanks."

For several minutes they rode in silence. Then she turned toward him and saw the set expression on his face. "What is it, Mark?"

"You're in danger because of me. I never meant that to happen." He nearly spit the words out. "If you're thinking of splitting, forget it. It's my responsibility to protect you now."

"I'm not." She sighed then. In a low voice she began speaking again, because when she'd been alone in the second bedroom, she'd been brutally honest with herself and now she knew she had to fill in the rest of the picture for him. "Maybe the danger reaches a little farther back. I've been going over a lot of stuff in my mind, trying to think about what was happening when Veronica was killed. I keep thinking Phil could have been involved."

"Yeah, maybe," Mark said slowly. He eased to the side of the road, then reached in the back seat and pulled up the carryall.

When he brought out the puzzle box, her eyes widened. "How... Where did that come from?"

He looked smug. "From the bad guy's car."

"You knew it was there?"

"No. But I told you I saw these goons arrive in the parking lot. The lot was lighted, and as soon as they pulled in I thought I recognized their car. I realized I had seen it in your neighborhood yesterday when that guy attacked you. I didn't think anything about it then. It was just one of the vehicles on the street. But when the same car showed up again, I figured it wasn't a coincidence so I checked out the vehicle.''

She reached for the box and turned it in her hand. ''So you're saying that the guy who attacked and robbed me was one of the men who just came after us? And he still had the box with him.''

''Did you recognize either of them?'' Mark asked without answering her question.

''No. But then, they had on those masks.'' She heaved a sigh. ''I guess I didn't hurt him with the scissors as badly as I thought.''

''Don't beat yourself up about that. You held him off until I could get there.''

She nodded.

''Well, either they're freelancers or they're hired help. It could be that the one who attacked you earlier was supposed to turn the booty over to someone and didn't do it. Or he hadn't done it yet. Or it could be that they planned to force you to open the puzzle box.''

She turned the wooden box in her hand pressing on various places. ''But I haven't a clue how to get inside it.''

''They don't know that.'' He waved his hand toward the box. ''Why don't we just smash the damn thing and see if anything's inside.''

Her hands tightened on the polished wood. ''Are you crazy? It's a priceless antique. I can sell this thing for a lot of money. I may *need* to sell it if I'm short on cash.''

''I have plenty of dough,'' he growled.

''I'm not taking your money!''

"Why not?"

She made a small exasperated sound. "You know why."

She thought he might argue with her. Instead, he started the car and drove off.

"Where are we going?" she asked.

"I don't know. Part of me is thinking that it would be a good idea to get out of Perry's Cove. And part of me thinks we're very close to figuring out what's going on here."

She agreed with him.

"Where should we hide out?" he asked.

She considered their options. "There are plenty of vacant properties around here."

"Yeah, we were using one. But they found us."

"They can't check every place that's unoccupied. Doris must—" She stopped. "I think Doris is in this up to her ears."

"She is—if Garrison is. She'll be able to figure out anything that goes through the real estate office."

"I know about a property that's vacant but not on the market. It belongs to a woman named Gloria Yeager who goes to the same beauty shop that I do. She had to leave suddenly because her husband took a new job. She's planning to have her sister move in soon, so she left the utilities on. But the sister has been delayed."

"Okay, maybe that's safe. Where is it?"

Molly gave him the address. It was on the other side of town, and she gathered he didn't love the idea of driving through Perry's Cove. But she couldn't think of any alternative.

She could see he was thinking hard about something. Finally, he pulled onto a side road, then took the case with the mask out of the carryall.

"They're looking for two people who went away from that condo, one of whom is Mark Ramsey. Not Mike Randall." He gave her a quick glance, removed the disguise from the box and held it up in front of him. Then he opened a tube of glue and started dabbing it on his face. Using the rearview mirror to work, he began fixing the mask to his face.

Her breath clogged in her throat as she watched him. When the transformation was complete, she could only stare numbly at him. A man named Mark Ramsey had been sitting beside her. Now he was Mike Randall. But not exactly the Mike Randall from the old days.

"How does it look?" he asked when he'd finished.

She tried to speak and heard her voice go high and strained. "There's a place where it's not stuck down."

"Could you fix it for me?"

She should say no, but the word wouldn't come. Her hand wasn't quite steady as she reached for his right cheek and pressed the rubber against his flesh. The mask didn't feel like skin. It felt alien under her fingers. Yet it looked real.

"Thanks," he said, his voice almost as strained as hers.

"You...you need to do something about your hairline."

She reached up again, pressing at the edge of the mask and bringing a lock of his dark hair down over the line. "I think that will do," she murmured.

He caught her hand and held it. "Thank you for helping me. I know that seeing me like this has to be a shock."

"Yes."

"It's a shock to me, too."

She managed a small laugh.

"Molly—"

"Mark, I'm dealing with a lot of stuff right now."

"Yeah." He sighed. "We need to get off the streets. And you need to get out of sight." He looked toward her, then the back seat. "Would you mind lying down back there?"

"All right." She climbed out of the car and got in the back, brushing the dust off the plastic seat cover.

"Sorry," he said. "This Rent-A-Wreck could be cleaner."

She didn't bother to point out that they hadn't exactly rented the vehicle.

Mark started the engine, pulled away from the curb and headed toward town. She lay on her side, watching through the window. She couldn't see much, just the tops of trees and occasionally the tops of buildings that she recognized.

When she felt Mark's foot jump on the gas pedal, she tensed.

"What?" she whispered.

"One of Hammer's deputies spotted me. That guy named Cory Daniels who was with him when he caught us at my house. I don't remember him from the old days."

"He's been here about four years."

"So maybe he doesn't recognize Mike Randall," he said.

She might have tried to keep the conversation going, but all thought had fled from her mind as he kept driving at a moderate pace. Time seemed to stretch out like a reel of movie film unwinding. What were they going to do if the officer stopped them? She was sure that Mark didn't have a registration for the car. And what about his driver's license? It didn't exactly match the face he was wearing.

And, oh, Lord, he'd gotten a gun from one of the thugs. Obviously that wasn't registered to him.

When she pictured him being led off in handcuffs, she felt her throat close. He'd been locked up in a prison cell once before, and she could only imagine how horrible that had been. What would he do if he was taken into custody again?

Chapter Fourteen

Molly lay on the back seat, hardly able to breathe, feeling the car move smoothly down the street. If she were the one driving, she would probably be pressing on the gas pedal and trying to get away, even when she knew full well that the response was irrational.

Her nails dug into the edge of the plastic seat cover. She felt trapped, closed in, and she understood a little of what Mark must have been feeling since he'd arrived in Perry's Cove.

She'd been so angry with him. She'd felt betrayed when he'd told her his real identity. It was clear he hadn't trusted her at first, and that had hurt. But suddenly it was a little easier to understand his motivation.

He'd been accused of his wife's murder and convicted. As far as the law was concerned, he'd been guilty. They'd thrown him in prison with a bunch of hardened criminals and treated him like pond scum.

She didn't want to think what terrible things had been done to him, things that would change anyone. And now he was sitting in a stolen car with a cop following down the street in back of him.

He must feel as if a trap was closing around him, yet he kept moving at a normal pace.

She opened her mouth, then closed it again. She wanted to say something reassuring, but there was nothing she could say that would make any difference.

Aeons seemed to pass as she lay there in the darkened car. Then from the front, she heard him breathe out a quick sigh.

"What?" she asked.

"He turned down a side street."

"Thank God." She couldn't stay lying down any longer. Sitting up, she focused on the back of Mark's head. She wanted to tell him what she was feeling, yet she knew this wasn't the right time and certainly not the right place.

"You think Hammer's involved?" she asked. "Or Daniels?"

"I don't know whether Hammer is in it," he answered. "I don't know whether he sent Daniels after me. But at this point I can't take a chance on trusting anyone in town."

Her stomach clenched.

"Except you," he added in a gritty voice.

"Oh!"

Before she could catch her breath, his tone turned businesslike. "Give me that address again."

She told him where the house was, then forced herself to lean back against the seat. She wasn't sure what to say to him now. One thing she knew for sure—she didn't want it to be the wrong thing.

A few minutes later he cruised slowly down Gloria's street. It was almost midnight now, and they didn't pass any other cars as they headed for her friend's house. She lived in an upscale area, where the well-tended lots were large and the houses were fairly far apart.

Molly pointed toward the house. "There's a long driveway. You can park around back."

Mark pulled the car to the rear of the house, where it was hidden from view, and cut the engine.

"Do we break in, or did she leave a key?" he asked with a wry note in his voice.

"You're getting kind of cynical," she murmured.

"It comes with the territory," he answered, and she could tell from his tone that the stress was getting to him.

Keeping her own voice neutral, she answered, "Gloria asked me to evaluate the property for her. She told me the key was under the big hydrangea bush near the back door."

Mark collected the carryall, and they climbed out. Without waiting for him, she headed for the door.

He caught up with her and grabbed her arm, none too gently. "Wait!"

"What's wrong?"

"I don't know. But I'm not taking a chance on your getting hurt. For all we know there could be somebody inside."

She doubted that was true, but she deferred to his judgment, hanging back while he found the key, unlocked the door and stepped inside. He returned in a couple of minutes. And, she noted immediately, he'd taken off the mask.

"Come in."

Lucky for them, the house was furnished. Mark lowered the shades before he turned on a light.

It was a large house, with a country kitchen, a family room and a more formal living and dining area.

"I see your friend left a computer on the desk in the office," Mark said as he stood in the middle of the living area.

"You want to use it?"

"Yes. To check on Doris Masters, among other things."

Molly wasn't surprised. It seemed likely that Doris was the reason for their unexpected visitors this morning. "Okay," she agreed, offering him the use of equipment that didn't belong to her. But then she'd offered the whole house.

"Did Doris give you any information about herself, about the time before she arrived in town?"

Molly thought about what Doris had said to her while they'd worked at Shoreside Realty. "She didn't really talk about her background."

Mark nodded and turned down the hall. She was as curious about Doris as he was, and she might have followed him into the other room, but she sensed his tension and figured that it was better to give him some space.

Instead, she picked up the puzzle box and sat down on the sofa. Phil had acted as if the antique was important. But so far she'd made no progress in figuring out the combination that unlocked it.

She wasn't sure how long she sat there with the box in her hands.

Some time later Mark came back into the living room, his shoulders stiff and a set expression on his face.

Molly raised her eyes to his. "Did you find out something incriminating about Doris?" she asked.

He snorted. "Not likely. Your friend Doris Masters

appears to have arrived in Perry's Cove three years ago. Before that, I can't get a line on her."

"She's not my friend," Molly answered immediately.

"Whatever," he growled. "The point is that when I did a background check on her, I couldn't find any records of her existence before the time she showed up here. Zero. Zip. Which means that Doris Masters is a false identity."

She digested that. "Why?"

"Your guess is as good as mine. Maybe she's an ex-con starting over here." He swiped a hand through his hair in frustration. He sounded as if he was on the edge of losing it. "I sent a message to the Light Street Foundation, asking if they could help me. But I haven't gotten a reply yet."

He began to pace back and forth across the room, and she knew that he must be feeling blocked at every turn. Nothing had worked out the way he'd thought it would since he returned to Perry's Cove. He'd been stalked, beaten, attacked and warned to get out of town.

When his gaze settled on the puzzle box in her lap, he stopped pacing and wedged his hands on his hips. "You're still trying to open that damn thing?"

"Yes."

"You think Phil left it for you because there's something important inside?"

"I don't know." She looked down at the box in frustration, giving it a hard shake. She thought again she should just take a hammer to it. Only it was too valuable for that, and it had been a gift from her husband. One of his last gifts.

She looked up and saw Mark striding across the room toward her. He stopped a few feet from the sofa.

"Phil told you he bought the box," he said. "Actually, when I first looked at it, I knew it was one that had belonged to Veronica. I remembered the damage on the bottom."

She stared at him, wondering if she'd heard correctly. "It belonged to your wife?"

"Yes."

"How could that be? I mean, how could it have been hers then Phil's?"

"I'd like to know. I guess she and Phil had some kind of relationship."

"You mean they were lovers? I'd have sensed if Phil were having an affair with someone."

"Would you?" he pressed.

She reconsidered her previous statement. "I thought I knew him..." Her voice trailed off.

"Well, maybe it wasn't something sexual. Maybe, like you said, they were in the Mike Randall conspiracy together. The box is as much mine as yours, so why don't you let me have a crack at it," he clipped out.

From the expression on his face, she knew that his thoughts had taken the same path as hers a few minutes earlier. Only she hadn't been serious about cracking it open.

"No!" She folded her arms around the box, but he easily snatched it out of her grasp. As soon as he had possession of the object, he hurled it across the room. It hit the kitchen wall and splintered, the pieces scattering to the tile floor.

Molly screamed as she saw the box fly apart. Leaping up, she sprinted across the room, then stopped dead as she stared down at the pieces.

Parts of the box were still intact. A kind of numb acceptance settled over her as she gingerly picked up a corner where two sections were joined.

Behind her, Mark uttered a curse. "I shouldn't have done that."

She heard his footsteps cross the room but she didn't turn. From the corner of her eye, she watched him squatting to examine the ruin he'd created. When he lifted the corner piece from her fingers, she offered no resistance.

For several moments they were both silent. Then he made a strangled sound. "It's not an antique."

"What?"

"Look at it." He turned the piece so that the interior surface was facing her, and she saw the construction technique. An antique piece would have been joined by tongue-and-groove construction. Instead, there were small wooden wedges holding the sides together.

"At least I didn't break a priceless piece of art," he muttered, reaching for more sections of wood. "It was a clever fake. They even made it look like some old ivory inlays were missing."

She picked up several pieces, searching for the places where the box would have slid open when the right combination of panels was pressed. She saw none. Mark seemed to be executing the same maneuver.

"It looked like a puzzle box, but it wasn't made to open," she finally said. "I mean, I couldn't get any sections to slide because there weren't any. So I guess there wasn't anything inside after all."

She moved so that she was sitting on a throw rug.

Leaning back against a sideboard, she turned one of the pieces in her hand, feeling tears gather in her eyes.

Mark came down beside her and touched her arm. "I'm sorry. I had no right to destroy your property."

She struggled to contain her emotions. Her grief over the last betrayal of her marriage should be private, yet she wanted to pour it out to Mark. "I was...I was so sure that...that Phil had left me a message. I guess he did. I guess he was telling me he wasn't coming through with any help from the grave," she said thickly. On the last word, she lost control, and a sob of grief and anger roared through her.

Mark reached for her and pulled her into his arms. She came to him, leaning against him, unable to do anything else.

He rocked her, brushed his lips against her hair, her cheek, and she accepted the comfort as she gradually brought herself back under control.

When the storm had subsided, she murmured, "Maybe smashing the box was a good thing. It shattered the last of my illusions about my marriage."

His fingers combed through her hair. "But I did it for the wrong reasons. I was angry and frustrated, and I took out my feelings on what I thought was an antique box." He gestured toward the pieces of wood lying near the wall. "I'm sorry. You must think I'm some kind of raving maniac."

She raised her eyes to his. "No. I think you're a guy who's had a lot of control snatched away from him. With your wife's murder and then the conviction and prison. But you wanted to be in the driver's seat again, so you came back to Perry's Cove with a plan. Only then, stuff started going wrong."

"It was a half-assed plan."

"It seemed like a good idea at the time."

"Why are you defending me?"

"Because I feel like we're finally speaking honestly." She swallowed hard. "And because I care about you."

"I thought you were finished with me," he said, his voice cracking as the words ended.

Her hands stroked his back and shoulders, feeling his strong muscles quiver under her touch, and she knew that she had the power to affect him deeply. "So did I," she murmured. "I guess I've changed my mind."

"Just now?"

"In the car, I think. When you saw Cory Daniels and you kept driving at a normal speed."

"I was wishing like hell you weren't in the back seat."

"Why?"

"I didn't want you getting into any more trouble than you're already in."

"I don't feel like I'm in trouble. Not now."

"You are."

"No," she answered, knowing the response wasn't exactly rational. She was in big trouble. But all she wanted to do was push the doubts out of her mind. So she brought her mouth to his, a light touch that began as a healing balm but quickly built in passion as each of them increased the pressure.

She opened her lips, and Mark made a low growling noise as his tongue entered her mouth and stroked against hers.

She had been angry with him, hurt that he couldn't see fit to trust her. Now all she wanted to do was cling to him. She closed her eyes and folded him tighter in her embrace, wanting to say so much more, yet sure the best way to tell him her feelings was through her actions.

The kiss went on and on, sealing them together with a blast of heat, until they broke apart, both gasping for breath.

He wrapped his arms around her and leaned back, lying on the rug and pulling her full length on top of him.

She pressed her head to his shoulder, then adjusted her body against his so that his erection was right where she wanted it—in the aching cleft between her own legs.

When she moved against him, he made a pleading, incoherent sound.

"Yes," she answered, the response purely automatic because passion was quickly taking her beyond words.

"Too much," he gasped, rolling to his side, lessening the intensity of the contact, even as his breath sawed in and out of his lungs.

She felt him trembling, felt him struggling for control as he pressed his face into her hair.

"Don't hold anything back," she managed to say. "I want everything you have to give me." As she spoke she reached between them and found one of the buttons on his shirt. With unsteady fingers she slipped it open and then another, so that she could reach inside and flatten her hand against his chest, feel the frantic beating of his heart. It gave her a sense of power to know that she was stirring him so deeply. Yet at the same time she felt humble. He had needed her, and he hadn't been afraid to admit that to her.

Now she needed him just as much.

He seemed to know that. He brought his mouth back to hers for a savage kiss, even as his hands pushed up her knit top and then her bra.

When he clasped her breasts, she heard a small sound of pleasure rising form her throat. And again he was right with her, his fingers finding her stiff nipples and building her arousal to an even higher plateau.

She gasped out his name, desperate as she found the buckle of his belt. When she'd freed him from the confines of his clothing, she took his hot, hard length in her hands and stroked him with a possessiveness that shocked her.

''Now. Do it now,'' she gasped, even as he slid her slacks down her body, taking her panties with them.

He might have struggled out of his own slacks, but she didn't give him the option. Desperately, she rolled to her back, then brought him to her, a small sob breaking from her lips as he entered her.

Her hands glided under his shirt, over his naked back, clasping him to her, then slid down under the edge of his slacks to his buttocks, her fingers digging into his flesh as he began to move inside her.

It was a wild, frantic ride. She reached her peak quickly, crying out as her orgasm ripped through her. She felt him join her in the stratosphere, heard his shout of masculine pleasure.

He clasped her to him, rolling to his side as he held her in his arms. She closed her eyes, drifting on a warm wave of contentment as he held her. But when several minutes passed and he said nothing, she raised her face toward his.

His gaze was fixed, as though he was staring at some scene she couldn't see.

''It's okay,'' she whispered.

He stirred and seemed to come back to earth. "What's okay?"

"Making love. It was something we both wanted. And I didn't give you any chance to back out."

"How do you know what I'm thinking?"

She reached to smooth a lock of damp hair back from his forehead. "It's a pretty logical deduction. You're thinking about when I found the mask. I was angry then, and I said things that were meant to hurt you. Now I want to be honest. I know we could have had an affair six years ago. But you were too honorable then. You're still honorable. You're feeling guilty about making demands on me. At least that's the way you're thinking about it. But you didn't make any demands. I gave to you—and took pleasure in return."

"It's not that simple. Are you going to let me get away with lying to you?"

"I understand why you did it."

"What about flying off the handle and breaking that box you thought was a priceless antique?"

"Yes. And we know it's not."

"That doesn't excuse me." He moved to get up, but she pulled him back into her embrace.

"We've got a bigger problem than a broken fake antique," she whispered.

"Yeah. Too bad the guys in prison didn't talk much about how an innocent man deals with a mess of bad guys."

SUNLIGHT WOKE Molly after much-needed sleep. Without disturbing Mark, who lay beside her, she gathered her discarded clothing and headed for the bathroom. There she used the facilities, then washed and finger-combed her hair.

As she did, she stared at her flushed face. Lord, she had never gone through so many emotional swings in such a short time in her life. She had fallen for Mark Ramsey. Made love with him. Been hurt and angry. Then forgiven him. Now she wanted to think that their shared intimacy several hours ago had changed things between them. But she knew in her heart that was wishful thinking. She had said she knew what kind of man he was, and it was true. He still felt guilty about lying to her, and about flying off the handle. But the problem went deeper than that. Until only a few months ago he had been in prison. She knew the experience had damaged him in ways that she would never understand unless he opened up with her. Really opened up.

Terrible things had been done to him, things that made it difficult for him to react normally.

She wanted to tell him that she had fallen in love with him. But she knew that would only make him feel more pressure.

Again tears sprang to her eyes. This time she fought them off. She wasn't reacting all that normally herself. She was a mess. And she wasn't going to get much better until they figured out who had set Mike Randall up and who was after Mark Ramsey now.

When she felt able to face Mark again, she started down the hall but found him in the office sitting at the computer.

"I got a message from the Light Street Foundation," he said, gesturing toward the screen. "They work in association with the Light Street Detective Agency. Apparently, one of their detectives, Alex Shane, had a case a few months ago where someone had appeared in a small town with a new identity. He said he'd check on Doris for me."

"Good."

"He may not be able to find anything."

"Don't make assumptions."

While she was standing in back of him, another message came in. It was from Bill Bauder.

Looking over Mark's shoulder, she read the terse words. "I have some information for you. Meet me at eight-thirty tonight at the *Voice* office."

"How did he know your e-mail address?" she asked.

"It was on the business card I gave Ray Myers when I was at the Sea Breeze Café. Probably everybody in town knows it."

"Are you going to go?"

"I'm thinking about it."

"It could be a trap."

"Yeah. But I need some damn information, and maybe Bauder will give it to me," he growled, then turned back to the computer screen.

"Okay," she murmured. After several seconds, she quietly exited the room. She wanted to tell Mark that if the two of them could just drive away from Perry's Cove and never come back, maybe everything would turn out all right. But she knew he wouldn't accept that solution.

He had come here with a purpose, and that purpose had taken on a life of its own. He wasn't going to give it up, not for her or anybody else. Even if it put him in danger.

She paced the living room for an hour, the way Mark had done earlier. Finally, when she felt like a pipe bomb about to explode, she marched back into the office. "You are not going down to meet Bill Bauder on his home territory," she shouted.

Mark whirled around in the desk chair, a startled expression on his face. "I wasn't planning to," he said.

"Just what were you planning?" she demanded, placing her hands on her hips and glaring at him.

He sighed. "I'm not planning to walk into a trap. I sent him back a message saying that I wouldn't meet at the newspaper office. I told him I'd let him know the time and place later. If he still wants to get together, he can play by my rules."

She breathed out a little sigh. "Good. Where are you meeting?"

"The old foundry."

She considered the location, picturing the redbrick building on the west side of town that had been a small iron foundry. The property was still in private hands, but the building was long neglected. "Why there?" she asked.

"Before Veronica died I was asked to evaluate the place as a possible retail venue. I've studied it. I can hide out and watch him arrive and I can stay undercover until I know it's safe. Does that meet with your approval?" he asked, an edge in his voice.

She nodded. "But I have one important demand."

"Oh, yeah?"

"If you're not taking me with you, you can't leave me here without transportation. I mean, what if something happens and I have to bail out?"

She watched several strong emotions chase themselves across his face.

"Let me work on that," he muttered.

IT WAS JUST BEFORE DARK when Mark got ready to leave. "Wait fifteen minutes, then send the message to Bauder with the time and place," he instructed.

Molly nodded tightly.

He knew that she wanted him to tell Bauder to forget it, but he knew just as surely that he had to keep the appointment. Nothing had gone right since he'd come back to Perry's Cove, but now he was going to change that or die trying.

He left Molly in the office, then headed for the kitchen to moisten his parched lips with a glass of water. A flash of movement made his head jerk up to see that she had followed him.

"I'm sorry," she said in a voice that wasn't quite steady.

He carefully set down the glass. "About what?"

"Saying you couldn't go to Bauder's office. Telling you I needed to have a car." She gestured toward the driveway where two rental cars had been delivered for a sizable extra payment by a company in the next town.

"It's okay."

"Mark..." She crossed the room quickly and wrapped her arms around him. Her face was against his chest as she said, "Please be careful."

He held her close.

"You're important to me," Molly whispered.

"And you are to me," he replied, his fingers combing through her silky hair. He wanted to stay. He wanted to tell her that he loved her. But he didn't have the right to do that, not after the way things had started after he'd come back to Perry's Cove—and not until he pulled himself out of the swamp that he'd waded into. So he contented himself with holding her for another few moments before easing away.

"I'll be back soon. Don't worry."

She made a small sound that might have been agreement. He forced himself to turn away and step through the door, feeling her eyes on his back until the door closed. Then he sensed that she had moved to the window, but he didn't look because he knew he might turn around and go back into the house.

Instead, he climbed into the midnight-blue Ford that the rental car company had delivered.

He had the carryall with him. It held the Glock he'd taken away from one of the thugs. He'd hoped he wouldn't have to use it, but keeping his appointment with Bauder unarmed seemed foolhardy.

Staying under the speed limit, he headed for the old foundry, then parked on a side street of moderately priced homes about a quarter mile away. Once, the building had been off by itself, but development had crept up to the edge of the property. That was one of the reasons he hadn't recommended using it for retail purposes. Even if the owners spent the money to get the building into shape, shoppers' cars would clog the neighborhood streets.

But now there was only residential traffic, and not much of that, he noted as he walked toward the building.

The weed-covered lot was fenced off, but there were wide gaps in the chain links big enough to drive a truck through.

The message he'd asked Molly to send Bauder had set the place for the meeting on the west side of the building. He arrived from the north and made his way around the structure, evaluating its condition as he went. The eight years since he'd done his study hadn't been kind to the property. Debris littered the grounds, and someone had sprayed graffiti on the walls.

He looked around at the site, wondering if this was really such a great location. But it was too late to change his mind now. Well, not too late, he reminded himself. He could still call Molly and tell her not to send the message to Bauder.

He could take her with him and just walk away from Perry's Cove.

The temptation to ask her again was burning a hole in his gut. Maybe she'd even agree to go. But he couldn't live with himself if he did. In prison, the guards had taken away his feeling of self-worth. When he'd gotten out, he'd decided that the way to get it back was to figure out who had set him up for Veronica's murder. He'd thought he could do it. Too bad it was proving to be more difficult than he'd anticipated. He'd come here looking for one guy. Now he knew he was fighting a conspiracy.

But that didn't change how he felt. If he gave up now, he'd be admitting defeat. And he simply couldn't do that.

His jaw set in a grim line, he brought his focus back to the building, looking for the metal stairway that led to the second floor. If it was sound, that was where he intended to wait for Bauder.

MOLLY LOOKED at her watch. Mark had been gone for thirteen nerve-racking minutes. Her fingers itched to send the message and get it over with, but he'd been specific about what he wanted, so she sat there waiting. Finally, the second hand swept past twelve, and she brought up the Notepad message Mark had written and pasted it into an e-mail to Bauder. Of course, there was no way to know when the newspaper editor would pick it up, but Mark was betting that he was waiting by his computer.

She didn't expect a reply, but she sat staring at the screen for several minutes. Finally she got up and wandered back to the family room where she'd long since cleaned up the pieces of the puzzle box. But she hadn't wanted to throw them away. They were in a plastic grocery bag that she'd found in the pantry.

Now, because she needed something to occupy her mind, she reached into the bag, pulling out some of the pieces and turning them over in her hands. She couldn't get out of her mind that Phil had made the box seem so important.

Maybe there was some clue etched into the wood, she thought as she examined the pieces. She didn't find anything on the outside. But when she turned over one three-inch strip of wood, her hand stilled. Taped to the interior surface was something she hadn't seen before—something that made her whole body go rigid.

Chapter Fifteen

Mark tucked himself into the dark recess under the stairs, pressing his back against the wall as he drew the gun from his belt and held it down beside his leg the way he figured an undercover agent might.

The light was fading, and he was pretty sure that Bauder wouldn't be immediately able to spot him hiding here. But the moon had risen, and unless a bank of clouds drifted across the silver orb, he'd have a good view of the newspaper editor.

If he showed up. There was always a chance that Bauder didn't like the meeting place and would choose to stay home. In which case, some rethinking would be in order.

Endless minutes passed, and Mark had almost given up when he heard the crunch of shoes on a place where the blacktop had crumbled.

Bauder walked hesitantly around the building, stopping a dozen yards from where Mark was hiding.

"Where are you?" he asked in a low voice.

Mark let him wait for several long seconds before answering, "Where you can't see me. Put your hands up. I've got a gun trained on you."

"How do I know that?"

"You just have to take my word for it. Put your hands up."

To Mark's satisfaction, the newsman raised his hands above his head.

"Why did you want to meet with me?" Mark asked.

Bauder shifted his weight from one foot to the other. "To warn you that poking into the Mike Randall problem could get you in a lot of trouble."

"Very charitable of you."

"I don't want to see you get killed."

"Why not?"

Bauder sidestepped the question and said, "Why don't you just tell Randall that you're risking your life by sticking around Perry's Cove, and you want out."

"Because I'm not the kind of guy who just gives up and goes away," Mark replied.

"Things have gone too far for them to back down."

"Them? Are you speaking as one of the group?"

"I'm speaking for myself."

"And who are your associates? Oliver Garrison, certainly. And Doris Masters."

"What do you know about them?" Bauder demanded.

"You called the meeting. Tell me something I haven't already figured out."

"Like what?"

"Like, is Hammer in on the deal?"

"No."

Could he trust that? Mark wondered. He didn't have a chance to ask another question. Before he could open his mouth, he was stopped by a blast of gunfire. Each shot registered separately on his consciousness. He counted five.

Bauder slumped to the ground in a pool of blood, as bright lights flicked on from somewhere, illuminating the area. Mark stayed where he was, hoping the shadows still hid him.

Silence hung in the air. He had just ducked farther under the stairway, when he heard another shot and felt a bullet whiz past his ear. If he hadn't leaned down at just that moment, he knew he would have been hit.

The sound of a car horn split the night. He looked up and saw a vehicle racing across the blacktop, headlights off. He knew he was trapped.

He raised the gun in a two-handed grip, prepared to defend himself. His finger was squeezing the trigger when he heard Molly's voice. "Mark, no!"

At that moment he realized that she must be in the car.

With a sick feeling in his chest, he lowered the gun as the vehicle screeched to a halt beside him. His hand scrabbled for the door handle. Then, he flung himself into the front seat.

Before he slammed the door closed behind him, Molly lurched away, making a tight circle around the now-lighted parking lot. Another crack of gunfire split the air, and another.

"Get down," Mark shouted above the pounding of the blood in his ears.

Molly ducked below the level of the dash, but she kept driving, heading for one of the holes in the fence. With her head down, her aim wasn't entirely accurate, and the side of the car tore against the cut edges of the chain links as it squeaked through.

As soon as they were free of the barrier, she took off, barreling down the street as though the devil were after her.

Maybe he was.

Mark looked over his shoulder. He saw another car gaining on them.

Molly made one turn after another, weaving through the neighborhood like a kid in a skateboard marathon. He kept his head and shoulders turned, watching their rear as she zipped down an alley then came out and made a quick right turn.

The vehicle behind them disappeared, and Mark let out the breath he was holding. "You lost him."

"Let me make sure," she answered, keeping up the same speed. A block later, he saw a side road that led into a scrubby area where there were no houses.

"Pull in there," he said, pointing to the narrow lane.

Molly did as he asked, driving into a narrow track that led across a large vacant lot. They came out in another development.

"Is Bauder dead?" she asked.

"He took five slugs. He was lying in a pool of blood. I can't believe he survived."

She let the answer hang in the air for several seconds before asking, "Is it safe to go to the highway?"

"I wish to hell I knew," he growled. Was it better to wait here, or take a chance on the road? "If we make a run for it now, there'll be one car looking for us," he said, thinking aloud. "If we wait, that could give the bad guys time to organize a posse."

"Then let's make a run for it," Molly answered.

"Okay."

She found the entrance to the highway and hesitated for several seconds before turning on her lights and heading toward their hideout.

He watched their back. When he was pretty sure they were home free, he switched his gaze to her. "What the hell were you doing there?" he demanded, struggling to keep his voice from turning rough. "You were supposed to stay out of this. I almost shot you!"

She glanced at him briefly, then fixed her gaze back on the highway. ''It came out okay.''

''Don't scare me like that again,'' he growled. ''What the hell were you doing there?''

''I came because I found a message from Phil taped to the inside of the puzzle box.''

That was the last thing he'd expected to hear.

''I couldn't throw the pieces away,'' she explained. ''After you left, I needed something to occupy my mind, so I started going through the wreckage, looking for some clue. There was a very thin piece of paper taped to the inside of one of the pieces.''

''But how? If we couldn't get the box open, how did Phil get anything inside?''

''The only thing I can figure is that he carefully took it apart then carefully put it back together.''

Mark thought about that. ''It must have been a lot of detail work.''

''He was a real craftsman when he wanted to be.''

''Yeah. I remember.''

''I guess he was feeling really ambiguous about the note. He wanted to leave a record, but he wasn't sure whether he wanted me to find it.''

''I wish he'd been more direct.''

''I guess he couldn't be,'' Molly said. ''He knew that if anybody found his record of what had happened, it could get me killed.''

Mark reached to squeeze her hand. ''Yeah. But now that you've found the note, you'd better tell what it said.''

''It said...'' She heaved a sigh. ''It said that there was a conspiracy to frame you for murder. Which I guess you already figured out. But there was other stuff, too. It said Bauder was part of it. That's why I couldn't leave you there.''

"You put yourself in danger!"

"So did you."

"You have Phil's message with you?"

"Yes, but I don't want to turn on the inside lights."

He nodded in agreement, then forced himself to wait. In the driveway of the house, she pulled up by the side door, opened her purse and reached inside. When her hand emerged, she was holding a small, folded strip of paper.

Instead of reaching for the paper, he reached for Molly, pulling her from behind the wheel and crushing her against him.

He clung to her with all his strength, and she held him just as tightly.

"Don't you ever scare me like that again," he said, his voice going low and rough.

"Oh, Mark," she murmured, her hands stroking his back and shoulders and hair. Finally, she raised her head, her eyes searching his. "I was right about Phil. He...was smack in the middle of it."

"That's not your fault, Molly."

She nodded. "Let's go in, and you can see for yourself what he had to say."

"Okay," he agreed, thinking that under ordinary circumstances he'd call the authorities and report Bauder's shooting, and the attack on himself and Molly. But these were far from ordinary circumstances.

She was standing nervously in the kitchen when he stepped inside and closed the door.

Better get it over with, he thought as he took the paper she was holding and walked to the light over the sink.

The writing was small and cramped, and it took several moments before he was able to make sense of it. Words and phrases jumped out at him.

The note was written to Molly. Apparently, Phil had been afraid to tell *anyone* the sordid story of what was going on in Perry's Cove. Yet he'd felt the need for confession.

Dear Molly,
If you are reading this, you have broken into the puzzle box. I'm sorry for what I have done. I got sucked into a situation that I thought would solve our financial problems. Instead, it's led to a trumped-up charge of murder against an innocent man.

Mark read that phrase again. *A trumped-up charge of murder.* What that sounded like was that Veronica wasn't dead—but that he had been framed for her murder anyway.

He continued reading.

They said Mike Randall would never go along with something illegal. Or maybe it was just that his wife and Oliver wanted him out of the picture.

He digested that and kept reading.

I let myself get swept along in their scheme. At the time it made sense. Then one day I woke up and realized what we'd done.

Mark stopped and thought about what he'd read. So Oliver had been having an affair with Veronica. He'd wondered if something was going on between them. But now Oliver had a new love—Doris Masters.

He read on, trying to take it all in. Phil had been deep into a plot with many of the other antique dealers, and other people in town as well, including Jerry Tilden. Jerry wanted to go from so-so builder to hotshot developer.

Phil had signed on to an elaborate scam. The plan was to buy the property where the antique mall was located and develop it as a high-priced resort. That was why they'd wanted it to look as if there were problems with the building, so it would make sense to tear the structure down.

They'd been working behind the scenes to collect enough money for a down payment by smuggling in fake antiques and selling them at the gallery.

Phil said from the grave:

> I asked why they couldn't just borrow the money from the bank. Apparently, they'd tried. But none of them had the clout to swing a bank loan. And they weren't seen as a stable enough group to hold together a consortium.

Mark digested that even as his mind flashed to the boxes he'd seen stashed in the vacant house. No doubt that had been a shipment of fakes.

He glanced up and saw Molly watching him.

"You got to the part about what happened to Veronica?" she asked, tension tightening her voice.

"Not yet." He kept reading, then sucked in a strangled breath.

> She wanted her husband out of the way. And she'd wanted to disappear and start over.

Start over.

As he grappled with that, the image of a woman leaped into his mind. When he gasped out loud, Molly took a step toward him.

"You're thinking the same thing I am?" she whispered as though she hadn't dared to ask the question until now.

"Doris Masters," he managed to say as his mind began comparing details. She weighed more than the Veronica he remembered. Her hair was a different color. Her face was different, her eyes wider apart and her chin bigger. She'd cultivated a different voice quality. But she was the same height. And there was something about her that had seemed as familiar as the landscape hanging on the wall in their old dining room. Only, the context had changed so much that he hadn't recognized the pattern. "Is it possible she did the same thing I did?" he asked, his tone matching Molly's. "That she had plastic surgery, made a bunch of other changes, and came back to Perry's Cove."

"I think so," Molly whispered.

Mark nodded in agreement. Even so, he was still struggling to take it in. Veronica had come back as Doris Masters.

"That fills in some of the blanks in the story Phil wrote me," Molly murmured.

"But there are a couple more pieces of the puzzle we need to fit into place. What about Dean Hammer and Cory Daniels?" he asked.

"Lord, I wasn't even focusing on them. I have good reason to hate the local cops. Do you think Hammer was so hard on me after Phil died because he's in on the conspiracy?" Molly asked.

He didn't give her an answer just yet. And he didn't tell her what Bauder had said, because he wanted her to consider the evidence on her own. He watched her gaze turn thoughtful. "I was jumping to a conclusion a moment ago," she said slowly. "But to be honest, I don't think Hammer was in on the plot. I mean, Phil wasn't the kind of guy who acted on partial information. He wanted to know every detail before he signed up for anything. I remember he drove Oliver crazy before we rented a space at the antique gallery. He had to nail down every detail from how far our space was located from the front door, to the average income dealers made per week, per month."

Mark considered the information. Phil had been pretty anal retentive, but that wasn't proof positive. "Bauder said Hammer wasn't involved," he finally admitted.

"When did he say that?"

"Just before they shot him. Which doesn't prove anything. Hammer could have been in on the deal and kept a low profile."

"No. Bauder would have known. He knew everything. But was he lying?"

Mark shook his head. "I wish I knew. Right now Hammer and Daniels are probably out at the foundry, trying to figure out what happened."

Her gaze shot to his face. "What if the investigation focuses on us?"

"Why should it?" he asked, fighting to dredge up air around the knot that had suddenly formed in his chest cavity.

"If Hammer's an honest lawman, he'll try to solve the crime," Molly answered. "And he might find evidence that we were on the scene."

A chill rippled over his skin. "Yeah, but what if he's not an honest lawman?"

"I guess he'd come after us, like the guys who

broke into the condo. But the conspirators didn't send Hammer. They sent a couple of thugs,'' she added quickly, probably in response to his queasy look.

''Yeah.'' His mind jumped back to her first scenario. An honest lawman going after criminals. Mark told himself he hadn't done anything illegal tonight, then quickly amended the assessment. Well, besides carry a gun that didn't belong to him and leave the scene of a crime. What if Hammer *could* figure out he'd been there? What if he got framed for another murder? He didn't want to be within a hundred miles of the sheriff or his deputy. Yet he didn't want Dean Hammer going after him again.

Probably Molly could see the warring emotions on his face. ''You could set up a meeting with Hammer, and I'll cover you,'' she said.

''I'm not letting you—''

She cut him off with a wave of her hand. ''Don't go back to that line about my not being involved. Not after reading that note.''

He nodded. ''Okay, let me think about it. I'm not going to meet with Hammer unless I think the odds are in our favor.''

IT HAD TAKEN Mark a full twenty-four hours to set things up the way he wanted. This time he was being smart, he told himself, hoping it was true. It was dark as pitch when he got into position in front of the Thompson house where he and Molly had found the boxes.

She was behind him in the sand dunes, as safe as she could be under the circumstances. But the knowledge that she was here at all twisted his gut.

According to plan, he and Molly had come in separate cars. She had gone straight to the house, parked around back and gotten into position in the dunes. He had found a phone booth at a gas station on the highway and made a terse call to Hammer, saying that he wanted a meeting.

When the sheriff had tried to question him, he'd given the meeting place then hung up.

He shifted from foot to foot, waiting for a police cruiser to appear. The wind was picking up, and he wished he'd listened to a weather report. He was pretty sure a storm was coming. But how bad and how soon?

When he caught the glint of headlights around a curve in the access road, he tensed and kept himself from looking toward the spot where he knew Molly was hiding.

The wait had seemed endless, but now that the moment had arrived, he had to force himself not to turn and run.

Hammer cut the engine but left the lights on to illuminate the scene. Then the driver door opened, and the sheriff heaved his bulky body onto the pavement.

"Ramsey?"

"Yeah."

The wind seemed to snatch the syllable out of Mark's mouth. Debris went whipping past the other door of the cruiser as it opened and Deputy Cory Daniels joined his boss.

"You wanted to talk?" the sheriff asked.

"Alone. What's your deputy doing here?" Mark asked, struggling to keep the edge of fear out of his voice. If there was anyone in the sheriff's department he didn't trust, it was Daniels.

Hammer didn't have a chance to answer.

Instead, Daniels shouted, "He's got a weapon."

In a flash of movement, Mark saw that both men had drawn their guns. And he was certain that he had made the final mistake of his life.

Chapter Sixteen

Mark threw himself behind a concrete planter.

Two shots rang out.

When he heard Molly scream, only one coherent thought remained in his brain. He'd failed her.

"Get down," he shouted.

In the next moment a harsh voice cut through the sound of the wind wailing and the fear clogging his brain. "Hold it, Ramsey," Hammer growled. "I nailed the SOB."

Mark's gaze zeroed in on the sheriff. He was kneeling beside the still body of the deputy. "Daniels is dead," Hammer said as he looked up. Mark saw raw emotions chase themselves across his lined face. Shock, sorrow, anger, regret. Like all the stages of grieving for a loved one compressed into seconds.

He stared at the sheriff, trying to clear the confusion from his brain as Molly tried to run toward him. A man standing behind her grabbed her by the arm and held her back.

"It's okay," Hammer said, his voice raw and angry as he stood up. "Daniels was going to shoot you. But I took him out first. Up until that last moment I couldn't believe he was going to do it." He fixed his gaze on Mark. "You're not carrying a weapon, are you?"

"No."

"Yeah, trust Daniels to shoot an unarmed man and claim it was self-defense. If I hadn't gone along with him, I would have been next. And he would have claimed we were actually working together on something dirty."

"What are you talking about?" Molly demanded. She was still holding the Glock Mark had given her.

Hammer, who had holstered his own weapon, eyed the gun. "Maybe you'd best put that away," he said dryly.

Molly blinked, then complied. Hammer switched his focus to the man who stood behind her. "Who the hell are you?"

"Dan Cassidy."

"The big-time lawyer I read about? The guy from the Light Street Foundation who got Mike Randall's conviction reversed?"

"I wouldn't call myself big-time. But I'm here now as Mark Ramsey's and Molly Dumont's witness to this meeting. And, yes, I'm from the Light Street Foundation."

Mark nodded to Dan, then swung back to the sheriff. "Want to tell us what just happened?" he asked, gesturing toward the dead man spotlighted in the glare of the police cruiser's headlights.

"I've known for a long time that something funny was going on in town and I was pretty sure Daniels was mixed up in it. But I didn't want to believe it, and I couldn't prove anything—not until tonight."

"You mean until you took a chance with Mark's

life,'' Molly said, her voice high and shaky as she raised it above the roar of the rising wind.

Hammer swung toward her. ''I had the situation under control,'' he growled.

Mark gave her a sharp look. They might still be reeling from what had just happened, but he knew one thing: questioning the sheriff's judgment wasn't the best policy—not when they were having this conversation over a dead body.

Hammer turned to Mark. ''Let's get out of the wind.''

Mark reached for Molly and guided her to the overhanging roofline of the house, thinking that was better than climbing into Hammer's cruiser. Dan Cassidy followed.

When they were somewhat sheltered from the weather, the sheriff said, ''You came to town to figure out who set up Mike Randall. I want to know what you've found out.''

Mark's mouth hardened. He looked at his lawyer. Cassidy gave a small nod, letting him run the show for the time being. ''If you put it that way, nothing,'' he said.

The lawman looked at him. ''You realize I'm going to have to explain what happened here. I'd appreciate something coherent to tell the state police.'' He looked at each of them in turn. When Cassidy kept silent, he focused on Mark again.

He considered the sheriff's position. He wanted to ask the man how it felt to be on shaky ground with the law, but he figured it was better to keep the question to himself. Better to consider his own position. He'd been at a disadvantage since he'd come back to Perry's Cove. But with a dead deputy lying on the ground, for the first time he felt as if he had some leverage. "You go first," he said. "Tell me why you suspected Daniels."

The sheriff's eyes narrowed. "This is a small department. I have to operate with reduced manpower. When I got wind that illegal merchandise was moving through the area, I put Daniels on it. He'd be out on patrol and come up empty-handed. I thought it was bad luck. Then—" He stopped and heaved a sigh. "It tears up your insides when you start to suspect someone you trusted has gone bad. Someone who's supposed to be watching your back. You don't want to believe it at first. Then you start to believe."

Mark nodded. "Who else did you think was involved?"

"Oliver Garrison. His girlfriend, Doris Masters. Bill Bauder. Jerry Tilden."

"That matches the suicide note that Phil left Molly."

The sheriff's gaze zeroed in on her. "You've been withholding information all this time?"

"Certainly not!" Cassidy interjected. "Her husband hid the note inside an antique box. They found it yesterday."

"Before or after the meeting with Bauder?" Hammer asked.

"When I was waiting for Mark to come back," Molly said, then clamped her hand over her mouth. "Sorry," she muttered.

Hammer's gaze drilled into Mark. "So you were there last night?"

"*I* was there," he said, emphasizing the pronoun, thinking that he could be writing himself a ticket back to prison. "Are you going to frame me for Bauder's murder?"

"I'm not in the habit of framing innocent people."

He almost said, "Funny, you could have fooled me." But he kept the angry words locked in his head. Instead, he gave Hammer a quick summary of what Phil had said in the note.

The lawman stood silently, taking it in, and Mark wondered if he was going to accept the story.

After several tense seconds, Hammer cleared his throat, glanced at Cassidy, then gave Mark a direct look. "Well, that explains a lot. Like how Mike Randall got railroaded into prison."

Mark felt light-headed. Six years ago, Hammer had been sure of his guilt. Now was the man really saying he'd been wrong?

"So you believe us?" Mark asked carefully.

"It's a wild story but it fits."

"Yeah, well, there's one more piece of the puzzle we figured out," Mark said. "The reason you never found Veronica's body is that she's not dead. She arranged to make it look like her husband killed her. Then she came back to town with a new face and a new identity. If you want to scoop her up, go arrest Doris Masters."

Hammer's jaw dropped open. When he closed it again, he said, "You're claiming that Doris Masters is Veronica Randall? But how?"

"She had plastic surgery. She changed her face, made her eyes look different. She gained weight and she dyed her hair."

"That's a lot to swallow—someone changing their looks so much that none of their former neighbors and associates recognizes them."

Mark laughed. "Then I suppose you're not willing to believe that you're talking to the former convict Mike Randall, come back with a brand-new face."

"What the hell...?"

"I'm Mike Randall—with a different face." He touched the fingers of his right hand to his cheek, the side of his nose, the corner of his eye.

Hammer stared at him. "That's crazy! If you expect me to believe that, you must think I'm soft in the head."

"Think about it, Sheriff. I wanted to find out who framed me for murder. And I wanted to do it in secret. What better way to poke around town without being recognized?" As he spoke, he worked hard to create his old voice.

Hammer goggled at him, took a step closer, then inspected him more closely in the headlight beams. Long moments of silence passed before he said, "Maybe I can see it, now that you clued me in."

"I planned it carefully, just like Veronica did," Mark said. "I came back to find out who killed her. Instead, I found out that she's not dead and that she and her friends are working overtime to protect a moneymaking scheme gone bad. It looks like they killed Bauder because he'd had enough and wanted to get out. They tried to kill me and Molly," Mark added, recounting the break-ins at the condo and at Molly's house.

"You've had an exciting couple of days," Hammer muttered.

"Unfortunately," Mark answered. "The only good news is that you're not in on the conspiracy."

Hammer's face hardened. "I've been working overtime to get these scum."

"You have to admit, it looked like you and Bauder were pretty friendly."

"Yeah, well, that's what I wanted him to think." He shifted his weight from one foot to the other. "Now I have to call the state police and report this shooting." He gestured to Daniels's body. "I assume the three of you will back up my account of the incident?"

"Yes," they all answered.

Hammer fixed Mark with a direct look. "I'm sorry I played a part in sending you to prison."

Mark could only answer with a nod. He wasn't about to tell the sheriff there were no hard feelings.

"I hope I can make amends by rounding up the bastards who did this to you. The trouble is, we still don't have the proof we need to arrest them."

"We'll get it," Mark said, thinking of the plan he and Dan had already started discussing. For long seconds he considered the wisdom of his next words, then decided to make a stand. "You owe me for what happened with Veronica," he said. "Why don't you go about your business and we'll go about ours? I mean, I'll call you in if I need you to mop up after we get taped confessions from those responsible."

Hammer's eyes narrowed. "You mean, forget we ever had this conversation about nailing the suspects?"

"Yeah." Mark held his breath, waiting for a response, watching Hammer's deadpan expression. One thing he'd learned tonight, the sheriff would make an excellent poker player.

Finally the lawman cleared his throat. "I guess I owe you one."

"Thanks," Mark answered.

Hammer turned to Dan. "I assume that as his lawyer you're not advising him to do something that will get his ass killed."

"That's right."

Hammer gave him a nod, headed back to his cruiser and reached for the phone.

WAS HE CRAZY? Mark wondered as he sat in his car at the far edge of the antique mall's parking lot, his vehicle partly hidden by low-hanging branches. It was almost dark, but he could see the wind whipping stray trash across the blacktop.

Climbing out of the car, he took a deap breath. He would have liked better weather for this confrontation, but he hadn't dared put it off. The longer he waited, the more chance there was that Garrison and company might take the money they'd collected and bail out.

As he walked toward the building, Mark stroked the rubber surface of the mask he wore. The mask that turned him back into Mike Randall. It felt firmly attached to his face, but it didn't feel real. It wasn't just the thin layer of rubber. A long time ago he had been Mike Randall. He'd changed too much to ever go back to that persona. Mike Randall had been too trusting, too clueless, too soft. Mark Ramsey was just the opposite. But was he also too reckless?

He stopped in the shadows, waiting with his heart pounding.

He'd worked this plan out with Dan and the Light Street Detective Agency—and Randolph Security. Light Street and Randolph were joined at the hip, he'd discovered, because the head of the detective agency, Jo O'Malley, was married to Cam Randolph, who headed up the security company. And a good thing, too, because Randolph had the technical expertise to pull off this stunt that he'd conceived.

A car drove slowly into the lot. It was Jerry Tilden, right on schedule.

The builder got out and stalked toward the front door of the gallery, head down, his face grim as he fought the wind. Tilden was the most confusing piece of the whole puzzle. Seven years ago it had looked as if he and Veronica had been on different sides of a big zoning controversy. But according to Phil, he'd gotten in on the land scheme with the antique dealers. And now it seemed that they were screwing him.

Why? What had he done to them? Maybe he'd tried to grab too much of the profits.

Mark waited in silence, his pulse rate accelerating.

It was five minutes before another car pulled into the parking lot.

This time his stomach clenched painfully. Molly was in that car. The idea of her being here where hot lead might start flying made him almost physically ill. But all the arguing in the world hadn't stopped her from coming.

Maybe she had something to prove, the way he did. He wasn't sure. All he knew was that, unfortunately, she'd given him no damn choice.

He shot her a fierce look as she crossed to the building, sure that she couldn't even see him. He'd thought when this was over he'd be free to ask her to marry him. Now he couldn't even do that, because he'd suddenly found out that his wife wasn't dead.

Dan had told him that getting a divorce would be no problem. But it wouldn't happen overnight.

He hadn't discussed any of that with Molly. He'd

been too shaken, and too wound up with making sure neither one of them got killed.

He wanted to get out of the car now and order Molly to stay out of the charade. He could take her place. But he stayed where he was because he knew that being here was important to her. He knew she held the antique dealers responsible for sucking Phil into their scheme. And he knew she wanted them to know she'd found them out.

As he watched, she struggled toward the back door, battering her way against the damn wind.

The night before, he'd arranged to have a key made. She used it and disappeared inside. That was his cue to follow.

The wind tried to rip off his mask as he hurried toward the building. Shielding his face with his arm, he slipped inside, remembering the night Oliver Garrison had shot at him. But this time it was going to be different, he told himself.

He could hear people talking loudly, excitedly. He crept through the storage room, then positioned himself where he could see into Garrison's office. As he drew his gun and held it down beside his leg, he glanced at Molly. She was close to the door to the room, waiting in the shadows, and he fought against the impulse to pull her into the workroom and tie her up so she'd be out of this entirely.

"What do you mean you didn't send the message?" Garrison was saying, his voice going high and shaky as he spoke to Tilden. "You said you wanted us to stop the accidents at your construction sites and you wanted to talk about it."

Tilden's tone was harsh. "I'm tired of your bullshit. I didn't call this meeting. I got a message from you.

You said you wanted to talk about Mike Randall and that other guy he sent here to find out about the smuggling and the land-deal scheme. Well, you didn't spell it all out, but that was what you meant."

Doris Masters rounded on Tilden. Mark was still having trouble adjusting his thinking about her. She was Veronica. The wife who had faked her death to get him sent away to prison. He'd known she was self-centered. He'd known their marriage was all screwed up. He hadn't dreamed how far she'd go to get him out of the picture.

She was addressing Tilden in an angry voice. "You're full of it. What are you trying to pull? We had this plan all worked out. Mike would get convicted of my murder, so he would be put away. You'd get the contract to build the new development when we had the money to buy the land."

"Except now you're sabotaging my construction sites," Tilden shouted. "So you can put me out of business and get another builder."

"It's not us," Mark's former wife said.

"Then who?"

"Maybe that guy Ramsey."

"The accidents started a long time before he arrived in town."

"Right. Because your work was already crap. That's why—"

"Shut up. Just shut up," Garrison cut in, sounding as if he was losing it. "We're in enough trouble already. Stop spewing out incriminating information. Don't you see we've been set up? Somebody wanted us all together, talking about the situation."

"There's no way they can prove anything," Doris answered, obviously trying to remain in control. "Not about Randall, and not about Bauder. The guys who took care of him are in Mexico by now. So we don't have any loose ends.''

As if on cue, Molly stepped into the doorway, and Mark's heart was suddenly blocking his windpipe. Lord, what if something went wrong?

His gaze never left her as she paused beside a large, elaborately carved highboy.

''Actually, I'm the one who arranged this meeting,'' Molly said coolly. ''I want a piece of the action. I found a letter that Phil wrote me. He left me high and dry, and that's your fault. I want you to give me the money he would have gotten,'' she added, pitching her voice above the wind tearing at the outside of the building.

For heartbeats, her demand was met with shocked silence.

Garrison finally found his voice. ''Now wait a minute. You can't just come in here demanding a cut. You were never in the loop.''

''Fill me in,'' Molly murmured.

''Like hell,'' Tilden shouted. ''You're in bed with that guy Mike Randall sent to find out who framed him for murder.''

Garrison laughed, but the sound was quivery. ''In bed is a good way to put it, isn't it? What did your lover do—send you to pry information out of us?''

''He says he's willing to tell Randall he didn't find anything—if you give him a cut. He says he wants to back the winning horse and he thinks it's you.''

''I'm supposed to believe that?'' Garrison asked.

''Believe what you want,'' Molly answered. She fixed him with a hard look. ''My boss, Larry Iverson, sent me to inspect that building you were renovating, and a bucket of shingles almost fell on my head. Is Larry in on the conspiracy, too? Were you trying to get rid of me?"

Garrison gave her a scornful sneer. "You have an inflated view of your own importance. Iverson sent you because he was too lazy to inspect the place himself."

Tilden jumped back into the conversation. "Your tangling with those shingles is just a side issue. You got caught in their scheme to ruin me. But we're going to cut through a lot of extraneous crap right now." From his pocket he pulled something that looked like a portable phone. "This is a transmitter set to blow this place up," he said, his voice gritty.

Everyone in the room froze. All eyes, including Mark's, riveted on the builder.

"See, I got myself an insurance policy a couple of weeks ago. I've wired this place with explosives. If you don't agree to stop screwing with my business, I'm going to bring this whole gallery down on top of you. And lucky for me, the evidence will point to storm damage."

Mark blinked. Did the jerk really think that the authorities wouldn't find the evidence of explosives?

"I don't believe you," Oliver said. "You wouldn't blow yourself up."

"Try me," Tilden dared. "All I have to do is press a combination of these buttons." He gestured toward the keypad.

From his position in back of her, Mark could see Molly go rigid. Oh Lord, now what?

"We're going to get this straightened out," Tilden was saying. "Now, whose bright idea was it to make me look bad? And why?"

''Bauder. He started questioning your work,'' the woman who called herself Doris Masters said. ''He said you cut too many corners. He wanted to get a contractor whose buildings wouldn't fall down after twenty years.''

''Convenient. Blame it on the dead guy.''

Mark watched the scene in horror. Yet again, things weren't working out the way he'd intended. This time he'd thought he'd done it right, with help from the Light Street Detective Agency. But Tilden had pulled a wild card out of his pocket.

Mark had his own transmitter in his pocket. It wasn't going to blow anybody up. At least he hoped it wasn't on the same damn frequency as the other one.

With his pulse pounding in his ears, he pressed a button, then stepped out of hiding, putting himself between Molly and the angry people in the room. He needed to distract Tilden, and the words he heard coming out of his mouth were, ''Actually, it was my idea to screw you up,'' he said. ''So don't take it out on your buddies.''

People gasped, staring at him in the Mike Randall mask.

Tilden's mouth fell open. Doris turned white. Garrison reached into his desk drawer and came up cursing. The gun he'd used wasn't there. Mark and his friends from the Light Street Detective Agency had made sure that it wouldn't be.

''Up here,'' four voices shouted from the second floor of the building, acting in response to the signal Mark had given. Four men stepped out onto the balcony, each of them wearing a mask with the face of Mike Randall. They were also wearing bulletproof vests under their clothing, as were Mark and Molly.

The men were Alex Shane, Jed Prentiss, Lucas Somerville and Hunter Kelley, all of them with Randolph Security or the Light Street Detective Agency.

Now there were five Mike Randalls in the gallery. The original and four copies. And it was impossible to know which was the real one and which were fakes. The crowd of instant clones was enough to drive anyone mad. Mark had counted on that. Counted on causing a lot of confusion with the ploy. But it looked as if Tilden had already done that, Mark thought with a strange kind of detachment.

Tilden screamed, "No!" and pressed two of the buttons on his transmitter.

In the front of the gallery, windows shattered.

Mark, who had moved closer to Tilden, threw himself at the builder, knocking him to the floor. They struggled for the transmitter and another explosion rocked the loading-dock area. From the corner of his eye, Mark saw that Garrison had leaped across the room toward an antique chest, where he fumbled in the back and came out with a revolver.

"Molly, get down," Mark shouted.

Doris had already pulled a small pistol from her purse. She and Garrison raised their weapons and started firing at the men above them. Tilden dropped the transmitter, clawed his way out of Mark's grasp and wedged himself under the desk as sirens sounded nearby.

That was Hammer and his men. The one nonnegotiable condition the sheriff had imposed was that he be able to listen in on the confrontation.

The men on the second floor returned the fire from below.

Doris fell to the floor. So did Garrison.

Tilden stayed where he was under the desk, his arms over his head.

It was all over in a matter of seconds.

Mark took care to pocket Tilden's transmitter, then turned and dashed to Molly.

"Are you all right?" he gasped out.

"Yes. Are you?"

"Yes."

He held her close for several seconds, then detached himself. "I have to..."

"Yes. Go on. Hurry."

Crossing the room, Mark knelt by the woman who lay on the floor. Her face was pale, and blood seeped from a hole in her chest. Her eyes were dull, but they zeroed in on him.

"Veronica," he chocked out, finally confronting her after all the years of pain and suffering she'd caused him.

"Mike..." She was silent for several seconds, then whispered in a voice so low he could hardly hear, "You came...back."

He wanted to understand. "Why did you do it? Why did you send me to prison? I would have given you a divorce. Our marriage was over."

"I'm sorry..." she answered. It was the last thing she said. Her head lolled to the side, and the life went out of her.

He stayed there for several more seconds, thinking about what she had done to him. He wanted to hate her. But he knew there was a better place to put his energy.

He stood up and saw Molly watching him, her hand pressed to her mouth. He gave her a tight nod. Quickly he crossed to her, then pulled her out of the room and into a dark corner of the warehouse as uniformed officers burst through the door. Cradling her protectively, he stroked her back and shoulders, profoundly grateful that she was all right.

She was shaking. So was he.

Upstairs, the wind caught glass fragments and sent them showering into the gallery.

"Is the building going to fall down around us?" she asked in a voice she couldn't quite hold steady.

"No. The building's solid as Mount Rushmore. Tilden just got a lot of bang for the buck by busting some windows. He was faking. He wasn't going to kill himself, just scare the others."

"Okay." She took in a deep breath, as if to calm herself.

"You trust my judgment on that?" he asked.

"Yes."

"I screwed up again."

"You didn't know that Tilden had gone off the deep end."

"Are you making excuses for me?"

"I'm reassuring you that your plan was good. And it was vetted by the Light Street Detective Agency."

"Yeah."

"Besides, anyone can make mistakes."

He dragged in a breath and let it out slowly. "I've made a lot of them since I came back to Perry's Cove."

"You came looking for a killer. How could you know you'd uncover a conspiracy?"

"You're making more excuses."

She raised her face to his and looked him straight in the eye. "Well, if I am, it's because I love you."

The breath froze in his chest.

"So what are you going to do about that?" she challenged. "Walk away because you're still feeling guilty about not leveling with me up front?"

"Yeah, I still feel guilty. But I'd be a fool to walk away." He clasped his hands over her shoulders, pulling her closer to him. "Molly, I've loved you for a long, long time. I was half in love with you back when we both lived here and my marriage had turned into a wasteland. Then in prison I couldn't get you out of my mind. There were so many things I remembered about you. I'd go over and over conversations we'd had. Or I'd remember how much I loved being in your house. How much you'd made it into a warm, charming home. I clung to things like that in the nightmare world where every day was a struggle for survival. You are the single most important thing that helped me keep my sanity."

"Oh, Mark."

"Then I came back here and started off lying to you. And I threw your puzzle box against a wall."

A smile flickered on her lips. "Yes. Breaking that box was a nice symbolic gesture. For three years I thought it might be my hope for the future. I thought I might sell it for a lot of money. You proved that wasn't really my future. You are. And you did me a big favor by breaking that box. You put my doubts about Phil's death to rest. I understand what happened to him. I can let it go, and I have you to thank for that."

He stared down at her, his throat too clogged to answer.

"You've lost so much," she went on. "Five years of your life. Let's not waste any more time arguing about what you did or what you should have done."

He swallowed around the lump in his throat. "I am so damn lucky to have you."

"The feeling is mutual. If you want to know the truth, I thought about you, too. My life here hasn't been so great. Alone in bed at night, I'd make up fantasies about you, that you'd come back for me and we'd go off into the sunset together."

"You did?"

She swallowed. "Yes. So you see, we've been on the same wavelength for a long time."

"Then can we get the hell out of Perry's Cove?"

"What did you have in mind?"

"A small city. Probably in the South, where I can start a custom building business and you can start an antique gallery."

She smiled. "That sounds heavenly."

"We won't have to worry about money," he added.

"I'd live on bread crusts to be with you."

"Yeah, but steak is better."

They kissed again, then he heard Hammer calling his name and Molly's.

"Ramsey! Dumont! Where are you?"

"I think we're going to be in for some questioning," Mark muttered.

"Only, this time you have nothing to worry about," Molly assured him. "The sheriff heard the whole thing."